HIDDEN IN OUR HEARTS

ENTWINED WITH LOVE AND PAST

GARJ'S QUILL QUARTET

Made with ❤ on the Notion Press Platform
www.notionpress.com

TO THE LORD, OUR GOD!

Contents

Acknowledgements

A work of art that takes the blessings and support of many took form today. We are indeed indebted to pay our gratitude to not just one or two, but every single soul that guided us through. We remember the earnest and thoughtful guidance rendered by Dr. Janneker Lawrence Daniel who selflessly poured us with his immense passion. We also thank Prof. Ribi Caroline, whose help should not go unmentioned. Without the support of our family and friends this would not have been possible.

We are much obliged to thank all the special people who helped us to build this from scratch,

Firstly, my mom, Prof. Ambika Vaishnavi, and Lenin Marshall encouraged me, Vijaya Lakshmi and Subbiah were the ones who spent their valuable time reading my works and helped me to do better. (Aram)

To my Pa, Ma, sisters, and Hephz, thank you for being kind to me. Dear Lord, my best friend, without You, I'm nothing. (RachE)

To my mom, who always supported me in the best possible way she could, then my brothers who stood by my side and bore my torture in the making of these works. Special thanks to Durai, who was busy with his work but motivated me throughout this whole journey. Madame, my dearest friend, gave her support in the best possible way she could in my work (A Voyage in Pursuit of Life's Destiny). Last but not least Muthukkumar encouraged me at times I needed. (Gabii)

ACKNOWLEDGEMENTS

I am deeply grateful to my parents and my friends, whose emotional and financial support made this endeavor possible. Their patience, kindness, and faith in me have been invaluable. This book is as much yours as it is mine. Thank you all sincerely! (Jeffy)

Authors' Introduction

'A whisper of hope' is what **RachelEliud** pictures in her writings. She is a post graduate in English Literature and a student of Bachelor of Education. She also pursues Diploma in Language Training. Granted with the precious little light from God, her soul elates for her profound passion of creating art. Her other fascinations are doodling and poetry. She believes that through her creations, her messy little world can be reflected and that is how her purpose blossoms a form.

R. Aramvalarthasivagami is a Bachelor of Education student who has completed her master's in English Literature.

Her passion for writing started with her journey with a collection of poems in different genres, moreover, her dream gave her another path to express herself through short-stories.

The biggest mission of her life is to trail other people to live in admiration of their life. As she is a self-loving person, she wants to make her name to speak volumes. And with the support of the right people in her life, she is doing great in her dreams.

Paul Gabriel. C is a law student who previously completed a Bachelor of Arts at ST John's College Palayamkottai. He is from a city called Tirunelveli, which has a history for itself and is located in the southern part of Tamil Nadu.

This young man has a desire to create something after his name in the future as he pursues law. So, he took a step which will surely give him a view that he has never witnessed before.

He is very passionate about art and is interested in connecting with other like-minded writers. He also co-authored a love-based anthology. He considers this platform as the right place to express himself.

Jeffrin Matthew is a versatile writer with a passion for storytelling across multiple genres, including short stories, novels, novellas, and poetry. Currently pursuing a Bachelor of Arts in English in his third year at St. John's College, Palayamkottai, Jeffrin has honed his craft through years of academic study and personal exploration. His schooling journey began at Bell and Rosemary, laying the foundation for his love of language and creativity.

Residing in the scenic city of Tirunelveli, Jeffrin draws inspiration from nature, which aligns perfectly with his hobbies as a nature lover, musician, and singer. Through his words, he not only shares captivating stories but also expresses emotions that resonate deeply with readers.

He believes in the power of resilience, encapsulated in his favourite quote: "Broken crayons still colour... So, if you are broken, don't worry... You will shine for sure!" Jeffrin's work reflects this spirit, offering love, hope, strength, and beauty, even in life's toughest moments. Keep an eye out for his literary adventures—there's always more to discover through the lens of his words.

CHAPTER ONE

Whisper of Reflection

-By Paul Gabriel. C

Tic...Tic...Tic... the clock's second hand is ticking towards twelve; the minute hand also attempts to touch the twelve. All of a sudden, a tiny speaker in the clock spills out, and it says, "Now that the time is four AM, fear not, for I am with you; be not dismayed, for I am your God; I will strengthen you, I will help you, and I will uphold you with my righteous right hand. A biblical verse from Isaiah 41:10: After this bible verse, a pre-recorded prayer of a Christian preacher is heard. A person who's nearly 75 leans on a couch with a glass in their hand. In a nick of a moment, the hand loosens the glass down, and it breaks.

The sunflowers in the terrace garden turn their yellowish heads towards the sky. A person who's in his mid-forties walks into the house with a muscular body who's about 6.6 feet tall, wearing a white vestment. A black rope on his waist with a knot on its end comes to his knee. He has a dark moustache and a light beard, with a slight baldness on his head. He comes along with the other two. The person on his right looks similar to him in the way he dresses and in other ways. On his left is a man who is about 65 years old, wearing a half-sleeve checked shirt tucked in with jeans. A young boy comes in a hurry and invites him by joining his hands. "Praise the Lord, Aiya" (Church Reverend), replied the Reverend. The old man who's on the left says, "Aiya, this boy is the son of Joseph, who is the youngest heir of this family." John the elder son wishes him and makes him sit. A load of cars parks inside the compound with rented chairs. Two boys come out and start to arrange the chairs one by one. A lady walks with a tea flask in one hand and a paper cup in the other moves forward towards a corner of the parking lot, and keeps them in a chair. One after another, people well known to this family start to come.

An ambulance arrives with a freezer box. Two men carry that box into the house and place it in the centre of the hall. A person who is around seventy-five to eighty years old comes out of a room, has specs on his eyes, is clean-shaven, and has a thick moustache. He wears a lungi with a black t-shirt that says, "Expecting the unexpected." The old man, who's near the Reverend, murmurs in his ears, "He is Mr. Durai, founder and chairman of Unlocked Solutions Pvt Ltd. and husband of Deepika Amma." The Reverend moves a bit and gives some space on the sofa. Durai can't accept the divergence of his wife. There is an absolute silence in the hall. "Sir, I'm sorry for your loss, and please don't get disheartened; she is resting in the hands of her Saviour." Water droplets start to flow from the lacrimal ducts of his eyes. He tries to control them but he can't.

Two men who brought the freezer box brought a junction box and connected the wire of the freezer box to that junction box. Joseph, who takes one end of the table, and John, on the other side, bring the table from the bathroom to the hall. "Guys, watch it carefully," says the 65-year-old man. The nasolacrimal ducts of the sons (John and Joseph) start to throw the water; it comes from their ducts to the end of their jaws until the neck. Both the sons place the table near the freezer box, and two men out of nowhere come in aid of these two to take their mother from the table to the freezer box.

"Two weeks passed without seeing her. She inquired about me every single time she could see my grandma. I used to claim a palm tree to collect the toddler, or palm nectar, in the early mornings at my uncle's land. When I got down, there was no one. I was confused and searched by calling out their names. At that time, I could hear a rhythm that was made out of an ankle, and the fragrance of jasmine flowers filled my nostrils." (The thoughts of Durai crossing over at a young age.)

Simultaneously, Durai tries to step up. His two daughters-in-law come to help him stand and bring him near the freezer box. With water flowing from their (daughters-in-law) eye ducts, they say, "Maa." with a broken voice. John takes a chair and puts it near the freezer box. As everyone in the house gathers around the box, they can witness a gorgeous lady who's in deep sleep from a few hours ago, with her favourite pink and gold silk saree, gloves on her hands, and socks too, with a pink shade of lipstick, and with a traditional Indian coil hairstyle. Her finger still holds the name of her beloved, which is carved in a golden ring, which is her engagement ring. Durai sits in the chair next to the freezer box, and he fixes his eyes on his wife's deceased body. Drops of water start to roll from his ducts.

As she came out of the motor room, my eyes were blurred, but I could hear the sound of the anklet, which gave me a feel that was not used to me, and it made my hand and legs shake for some minutes. A girl who'd be around 5.6 and looked neat and pretty had a literate look and wore a purple half-saree, her hair braided in traditional style with jasmine on it. And a golden anklet on her leg and her neck carried a long chain with a cross dollar on it. I tried to move out of that place but couldn't.

Yes, uncle, suddenly this morning around 4 a.m., when Dad woke up for his morning prayer, he noticed a glass was broken and shattered on the floor and could see her slipping from the couch to the floor. Dad cried out loud by saying...

A hand on the back of his shoulder says, "Joseph, want a minute to talk?" John says, "Excuse me, uncle." "Sure kiddo." Yeah, John, what's the matter? "Where is George?" I can't reach him. I tried a couple of times, but I can't get him on the line. Do you know where he is?" asks John. "Before an hour, I received a message from Sherly Anni that they would be boarding on British Airways in half an hour."

While their conversation is going in this manner, the Reverend comes out of the house and walks straight in the direction where Joseph and John are in the middle of their conversation. On seeing the Reverend, they stop the conversation and say, "Aiya." Joseph responds immediately. Reverend asks them, "Which time have you guys planned for the funeral service? Is it today?" John responds quickly and says about his younger brother George, who is from the UK, and also says he'll be here before midnight. John continues by saying that many people from different states of the country have to come for this, so it'll be convenient for them to attend the funeral if it's tomorrow.

"Okay, then we'll conduct the funeral service tomorrow at noon."

Both brothers agree on the timing of the funeral service; their countenance bears and shares a witness to the absence of hope and faith. On seeing the countenance of both, the Reverend comforts with a verse from the Holy Bible, which is in Isaiah 49:15. "Can a woman forget her nursing child and say that she should have no compassion for the son of her womb? Even these may forget, yet I will not forget you." The words by the Reverend lighten up some hope in the souls of the brothers. The Reverend gets in his car, and the white Swift leaves the house.

Time runs faster than usual, and many poor people come to catch sight of the corpse, which had the most gorgeous soul once. Many talk in this way: "Even though she's a deceased person, nevertheless, her visage shows like she's in a sleep." It was almost ten in the night, yet his eyes never slipped off her till this moment; looking at him in this pathetic situation gave enormous pain to friends and his family.

She came very close to me, gave me a big slap across the face, and said, "Oh! You started to avoid me," I replied, rubbing my cheek, "no, no, not like that." She asked me, "Then what?" I told her everything that happened on that day. After that, we spent some time together, and she left.

Till the previous night, he has been like a lion who handles everything as a single person in business as well as in family, but now he's out of words and out of action, and of course, he has the name of livest but dead.

The late 1970s

Either side of the road was full of palm, coconut, and neem trees. An old postman who compelled his legs to cycle. Who comes once or twice a month? Once he entered our village, the cycle stopped at his regular place for tea. It was the only tea shop and hotel in our village. In the evenings, it was operated as a hotel and had the name "Muthu Viyanthar." After he got refreshed with that tea, he crossed almost every child in our village on their way to school. The cycle stopped at a hundred-year-old Banyan tree, which was at the centre of our village. The postman got down from the cycle, and the villagers who saw the postman surrounded the cycle and started to ask about the letters that were written to them by their loved ones. The image looked blurry. He was about 5.2 feet tall and running towards the crowd. When that image came closer to the crowd, it was none other than an old lady whose hair was white and whose wrinkled skin looked about seventy-nine. Behind her was a middle-aged man who had a broad shoulder and a big moustache that was twisted and had some grey hair. The old lady who wore a classic white cotton saree was my grandma. She came there and didn't join the crowd, as it sounded like a market. When the villagers saw the man with the twisted moustache coming towards them, they all stopped, and many unfolded their dhotis and folded their hands in front and said, "vanakkam Aiya" (greetings, sir), and the postman too. He was the head of our village, and my uncle was too. Then he replied, "Ah, vanakkam vanakkam," and inquired about whether he had received any letters. After getting the letter from the postman, he asked the villagers to be patient, and then it'd be easy for the postman to deliver their letters correctly. He moved for about five or six steps, then turned back and asked the postman, "Is there any letter for Amma or any for that useless fellow?" The postman looked for a minute or two and handed a postcard to him. He called the old lady Amma, "Here it is, finally your useless grandson Durai has passed the eleventh grade." She got the card and thanked God; she came back to the house. I was in a good sleep.

She called me "raza...raza..." to wake me up. I was like, "Leave me for just a few minutes, Aatha." She told me that I'd cleared my eleventh grade; it was great news for me because it took me five years to clear the exam. My grandma had a dream of me becoming a respectable man in society. As I was overjoyed, she gave me another sweet piece of information: that my cousin Deepika was returning home after the completion of her course. I jumped up and gave my grandmother a hug and a kiss on her cheek. She might have thought that hugs and kisses were for the exams. I was expecting her arrival and planned to pick her up at the Tirunelveli Junction (railway station) with my uncle. Uncle Samuel came out of the house with Aunt Mary, who was his second wife. The starting sound of the engine hit my ears. A classic navy-blue ambassador came in front of the house. I just opened the door for my uncle and aunt, and then I asked, "Uncle... shall I? "He suddenly replied, "You..." and never let me utter another word and said, "Don't you dare to come, even for the next 5 weeks?" With that, he used abusive language against me and also warned me not to fall into Deepika's eyes till she left the village. I went home, and my grandma asked about my dull face. I could only say, "Nothing. "My eyes were full of tears, and I went out wept for an hour, and returned home.

The time is about 1:23 AM. A white SUV approaches the gate, which has a logo as a roundel, and it divides the roundel into quadrants of alternating white and light blue colour, which also have the letters of BMW in the outer circle and X5 xDrive30d M Sport as the model's name on the backside above the registration plate. A man who is in his mid-thirties gets out of the car. Joseph runs out to the car, hugs the man, and cries, "George, Amma left all of us alone."

"What are you talking about? John said Amma was in a critical condition."

"No, she was..." As he is saying to his brother George, he can't control himself and starts to yearn and cry out in a high voice. John comes and comforts both his younger brothers with some words of hope and faith. Sherly, who's the wife of George, gets emotional, and tears start to flow from her eyes. She stands like a frozen mountain, with great disbelief on her face. Uncle Muthu comes and makes her feel better in the best possible way he can. The driver's side door opens for Paul, who's the other friend who calls the servants to take the luggage from the car.

I left my village three days after her marriage was planned and I was in the nearby town at my friend Muthu's house. On that day, we planned for Muthu to be at the bus stop, which was on the other side of our village, with a hired car before eleven-forty-five PM.

As soon as the car door opens, a small barefoot touches the floor, wears grey shorts with a suspender on top, and has a cap on his head. Sherly takes the cap off his head and takes him in her arms along with George to see her mother-in-law. George sits near his father's feet, holds his leg, and cries. Durai can hear the voice of George, but he can't respond. John's wife (Mercy) and Joseph's wife (Johanna) are sitting on the sofa when Sherly comes in. Mercy gets her bag, and Johanna takes Jaden in her arms. She brings Jaden near the freezer box; on seeing his grandma, he has a smile on his face and tries to get out of Johanna's arms. She lets him down and sits down near the freezer box. He calls her by saying, "Paati, Paati, Paati." (grandma...., grandma...)

I went home by night around ten past thirty, and as per plan, Deepika came to my home without any baggage by pretending that she was there to see my grandma. She was there when I entered my home. Grandma asked where I'd been for the past three days, and I told her about our relationship and our plan to elope. She told me, "You can't go through or bypass our village since there is only one way to enter and exit our village." Then I shared something, which made her frozen for a moment. We both left my home by giving my grandma a final hug. I got a bag with some of my clothes, a candle, and my certificates for two hundred bucks. My grandma was silent till I made my feet out of the house.

She called me and said, "Once you reach Chennai, send me a telegram." I replied, "Yeah, for sure."

He waits for a minute for her to respond, but with no response again, he starts to call her. This time he taps the freezer box and calls "paati vaa..., paati vaa..." Every ten individuals around here start to cry at the actions of this small boy. He comes near Durai and asks him, "Thatha (grandpa) calls paatti." Durai looks at him and tries to say something, but instead of words from his mouth, tears start coming from his eyes. Everyone tries to make him calm about doing something, but they can't do anything except cry. Suddenly, Mercy takes Jaden in her arms and goes out to make him calm. Meanwhile, Muthu and Paul try to make him calm by giving him some water. After some fifteen minutes, Mercy comes with Jaden on her shoulder, who's asleep and goes into the next room.

The next morning, my uncle's chief servant called and took me to the field. There were five other men. They assaulted me and warned me thereafter that if they saw me with Deepika, they would kill me. Their assault made our relationship even stronger as the notification of her job was delayed. We got our time for each other in secret places where my uncle could not find it. One day she told me that her father was planning her marriage, and before that, my uncle wanted me inside the jail or to be dead. We tried a lot to change their decision, but nothing worked out. So, we planned to elope.

As time passes, the morning arises, and the papers of the daily calendar rattle for fan speed. Sherly clips them with a binder clip, as the date of the 9th of October is now visible. Many relatives from faraway places and known people are willing to pay their last respects to the corpse. Mercy, with Jayden in her arms, feeds him by roaming around the first floor. John is too busy with his computer and leans on his couch with some frustration. "Appa, it's already 11.15; soon or less, I'll be here." He replies, "As our offices are on leave for these four days, drafting the mail to our clients." The mobile rings, and Siri, the AI, says, "Unknown caller." Mercy picks up the mobile and asks who's speaking. The person on the other hand asks about John; she hands the phone over to John and continues to feed Jayden.

At about 11:48 AM, a white Swift with a sticker named El-Roi on the windshield parks in the parking yard. Joseph guides the Reverend's family towards the house. While they are talking about funeral arrangements and coffins, an old classic navy-blue ambassador comes through the gate, and the church bell strikes twice, three times, to indicate death. The car looks in perfect condition and parks in front of the house. John runs from the house and opens the car door. A walking cane is made of wood placed on the floor and covered with gold on the handle. A man who is around ninety to ninety-five, wearing traditional South Indian dress with white hair and a twisted white moustache, tends to get out of the car with the help of John. The Reverend asks about the old man who gets out of the car. Joseph has no idea, but he manages to explain it by saying the old man is a distant relative.

She got into my uncle's land through the main gate, and a servant opened up the gate as a way to her house. I jumped over the compound wall, and we both went to the right corner of the land, where no one dared to go for years. She was terrified to step into that place; there was a prohibited well, which had many conspiracy theories. I lit up the candle, which let us go inside the well through steps as the well was empty. As we went about thirty-two steps, there was an old steel door.

It was just closed, and someone might often use it. This was a tunnel path that was used by the English Army men back in the 1930s and 1940s to get to the other side of our village. Nobody in my village knows about this tunnel path to date.

The land got into many men's hands and finally reached my uncle. The underground tunnel looked so big that I felt that some had used it in recent times. With the help of the candle, we went for about 3.75 km from the starting place. On our front, we saw a steel ladder that was attached to the surface of the tunnel, and it looked like a lid on top of it. I climbed the ladder, opened the lid, got out of the tunnel, and then gave her a hand to pick her up. We could see Muthu waving his hand; suddenly, a light stuck on my face, and I went down.

As the funeral is going to start, John brings the old man near the freezer box and makes him sit on a chair next to Durai. In the meantime, the reverend family pays their last respect by placing a garland. On seeing the corpse, which is like a bride ready to meet her groom, the old man starts to beat his head and chest and cries out very loud. Durai still can't accept Deepika's death. The voice of this old man distracts him and reminds him of someone.

When I raised my head, a person who wore a traditional South Indian dress came out from the blue ambassador. He took his revolver on his and pointed it toward my head and shouted, "On the very day when we killed your mother and father, I told the old freaking lady to kill you, but she wants to use you as a servant.".

The words he spoke never entered my ears. I was like, "How the hell did he come to know?". Deepika begged by holding his foot, "Dad, leave us; we'll never fall on your sight," but he was very stubborn and kicked her; she went about three to four feet with my bag. Till he kicked her, I was stunned, and by fear of death, once he kicked mine, I got angry. By crying out in a loud voice, I moved a bit on the front towards him. He pointed me at my chest; a kick by Muthu on his spine made him track my left arm. The sound made Deepika unconscious. I controlled my pain, and to wake her up, I tapped on her face, which let her open her eyes. Muthu tied my uncle's hand on the back with the Dhoti he wore, tied his mouth with his shirt, and ran towards the car before me.

Every family member has a question in their mind: "Who is this? I have never seen him before." George and Joseph call John to another room and ask about this old man. He instantly gives them the reply, "He is that person whom our mom told us about for years. Our Grandfather" The boys' overwhelming behavior brings out tears in their eyes as they come out of nowhere and hug their grandpa. These emotional happenings come to a pause as the reverend starts his prayer. The young chap Jayden with a "red ball" in hand taps the freezer box and calls his grandma, saying "Paati vaa."

And suddenly I could feel that someone was on my back. When I turned back, a knife just went an inch into my gut. A hand tried to push the knife onto my body. I held that hand and looked at her face. It was the lady who called me her grandchild.

Mercy takes Jayden in her arms, and he starts to cry by calling his grandma and throwing the ball, which falls on the face of Durai, who's like a statue without any sense.

As noon comes, the Reverend begins the funeral by thanking God for her life and then thanking him for the wonderful work of God through her in many people's lives. He asks God for hope and peace among the whole family. He adds some verses from 1 Thessalonians 4:14–17.

"For since we believe that Jesus died and rose again, even so, through Jesus, God will bring with him those who have fallen asleep. For this, we declare to you by a word from the Lord that we who are alive, who are left until the coming of the Lord, will not precede those who have fallen asleep.

For the Lord himself will descend from heaven with a cry of command, with the voice of an archangel, and with the sound of the trumpet of God. And the dead in Christ will rise first. Then we who are alive, who are left, will be caught up together with them in the clouds to meet the Lord in the air, and so we will always be with the Lord." As these words come out of his mouth, the tears flow like water from all the people in the room. He concludes the prayer "in Jesus' name, asking Father."

The prayer by the pastor gives us lots and lots of hope and a peaceful mind. Every person pays their last respect to a lady who has done her work on this earth.

When I saw that face, my heart shattered, and I lost my grip on her hand, which let her inch onto my belly. Deepika, with a shattered high voice, took some sand and threw it in her eyes, and that let Deepika push her down. I leaned on her lap, and as my eyes were going out, she tapped me on the cheeks. "Driver, faster...." Muthu cried in nervousness. I got treatment for several weeks at Muthu's house after we moved to Mumbai. There is a promise she made me that day: "I've always been there for you till the last breath of your life."

As everyone around there is filled with lots of emotions and pain, many are crying silently, as the droplets fall from their ducts. Durai's head falls as George runs near his father and tries to wake him by tapping on his cheek and chest.

After three soul-crushing days...

Prayer songs are heard through the speakers, and Biryani is getting ready in the backyard. Three in-laws sing the song of God, and Sherly gets up to pick Jayden up as he's crying after a nap. Mercy makes her sit and goes to pick Jayden up in Durai's room. She takes him in her arms and notices a customized dairy with an unclosed pen inside. Which has a cover of "Her Struggles to my success."

CHAPTER TWO

Dining with the Dead Couple

-By Jeffrin Matthew. M. R

As the last rays of the sun faded, and the moon began to rise, casting a soft glow over the village. I had just finished setting the dining table, ensuring everything was in its place. The house, which had belonged to my ancestors, stood tall and proud, the largest in our village, holding countless memories within its walls.

The only thing missing was the food. My friends were supposed to make it; we had planned this gathering to make the most of my parents' absence while they visited my aunt for a few days. The idea of hosting a dinner in the old house, surrounded by the familiar creaks and whispers of history, excited us. It had been a long time since we all got together like this, and this seemed like the perfect opportunity. As I waited for my friends to arrive, I couldn't help but feel a sense of nostalgia mixed with the thrill of the night ahead.

Out of the seven friends invited, four had arrived: Arjun, Inam, Rhenius and Riya. Inam and Riya, the 20-year-old twins, were nearly identical in appearance, with their only noticeable differences being their gender and voices. Inam was the spitting image of Riya, as if he were her reflection in the mirror. Arjun, who was a few years older at 23, was the natural leader among us, always calm and composed.

They pulled up in a car with Rhenius. Rhenius, the ever-reliable friend, was also part of our gathering, though his arrival with the first group had been quiet. He was the kind of person who often stayed in the background, but his presence was always felt. At 21, he was the unofficial sponsor of our group, the one who always stepped up to make things happen. Whether it was arranging a trip, covering for someone who was short on cash, or organizing our gatherings, Rhenius was the one who ensured everything ran smoothly.

As they drove through the tall, iron gate of the ancestral house and into the garden, the encroaching darkness made everything seem shrouded in mystery. The garden, which during the day was a vibrant patch of green, was now barely visible, its features lost to the night. The trees rustled gently in the evening breeze, and the shadows seemed to dance with the dim light of the rising moon.

I could hear the car doors slam shut and the muffled sound of their voices as they approached the front door. The anticipation of their arrival had been building all evening, and now, as they stepped into the house, the night truly began.

A little while later Shaun arrived. Shaun, with his round frame and ever-present grin, was the unmistakable foodie of the group. His love for food was evident not just in his appearance but in the way he talked about and prepared meals. He and Arjun were our designated cooks, a duo that could whip up anything from a simple snack to a feast. The rest of us often marveled at their skills, and tonight was no exception.

As they stepped into the house, I could see the excitement in their eyes. The idea of spending a night in the ancestral home without the usual restrictions had everyone feeling a little giddy. The silence that had filled the house until now was quickly replaced by the hum of conversation and laughter as the group finally came together. It was a rare treat to be free from the watchful eyes of elders, and we were determined to make the most of it.

The house, usually quiet and filled with echoes of the past, now filled with youthful energy. We were all between the ages of 20 and 23, caught in that sweet spot of adulthood where responsibility is still optional and fun is the priority. The night ahead promised to be one filled with memories—ones that would undoubtedly be recounted in the years to come with fondness and perhaps a little bit of nostalgia.

Anandh and Sana, the sibling duo, were the last to arrive. Anandh, the elder brother, had always been the responsible one among us. At 22, he carried himself with a maturity beyond his years, often the one we turned to for advice or when we needed someone level-headed. Despite his serious demeanor, he had a warmth about him that made everyone feel at ease.

Sana, on the other hand, was the youngest of the group, having just turned 18 last month. She was full of life, her charm radiating wherever she went. This was a special time for her—stepping into adulthood and savoring every moment of it. Her recent birthday had been a grand affair, a mix of childhood innocence and the first taste of adult freedom. Tonight, she was just as excited as the rest of us, perhaps even more so, eager to be part of the group without the constraints of being seen as the "younger one."

As they joined the rest of us in the living room, the group felt complete. The dynamics of our little circle were varied and balanced, each of us bringing something unique to the table. Anandh's calm presence, Sana 's youthful energy, Shaun's infectious enthusiasm for food, Arjun's quiet leadership, the inseparable bond of Inam and Riya, and the collective anticipation for the night ahead—it all blended together into something that felt like home.

The house, now filled with voices and laughter, seemed to come alive. We gathered around, settling into the space that had been prepared, ready to enjoy the night without the usual pressures or responsibilities. The freedom of being in this old, grand house, with no one but ourselves, felt like a breath of fresh air. We knew that this night, in all its simplicity, was going to be one we would remember for a long time.

As the night settled in, Shaun and Arjun took charge of the kitchen, moving with a practiced ease that came from years of cooking together. The aroma of spices soon filled the air, promising a delicious meal to come. The rest of us gathered in the living room, catching up on life and sharing stories, the conversation flowing easily among old friends.

Sana, however, was too restless to sit still. The house, with its grand architecture and rich history, beckoned to her.

"Hey, I'm going to explore a bit," Sana announced, her eyes gleaming with excitement.

Anandh glanced at her, a protective instinct flaring for a moment, but then he smiled, understanding her curiosity. "Don't get lost in there," he teased lightly, knowing the house could feel like a maze to someone unfamiliar with its many rooms and corridors.

Sana grinned back and then slipped away from the group, eager to uncover the secrets that the old house might hold. She wandered through the long hallways, her footsteps echoing softly. The walls were lined with portraits of ancestors, their eyes seeming to follow her as she passed.

As she reached the top floor, she paused at a large window overlooking the garden, now cloaked in darkness.

Back downstairs, the I, Anandh, Rhenius, Inam and Riya continued our conversation, occasionally glancing toward the kitchen where Shaun and Arjun were busy.

But in the back of our minds, we knew Sana was having her own little adventure, exploring a house that had stood as a silent witness to generations before us. It was a night for making memories, and Sana was determined to make hers just as special as the rest of us.

Inam noticed that Sana had been gone for a while and decided to check on her. He found her upstairs, standing by a large window, captivated by the view of the darkened garden below. Inam felt a quiet fondness for Sana, drawn to her innocence and the way she seemed to find wonder in everything around her.

As they exchanged a few words, Inam couldn't help but smile at how easily she laughed at his jokes, something she had always done. Her laughter was genuine and infectious, a sound that made him feel like the funniest person in the world. It was one of the many things he admired about her—how she found joy in even the smallest things.

Their brief time together only deepened Inam's attraction to her. It wasn't just her innocence that drew him in, but the way she brought lightness to every moment they shared. Sana, for her part, was simply happy to be in his company, enjoying the night with someone who understood her and made her smile effortlessly.

While they were talking, Sana confided in Inam about her struggles. Sana and Anandh had grown up without their father, and their mother, carrying the weight of raising them alone, had become focused on securing their futures as quickly as possible. For Sana, this meant her mother was eager to see her married off soon, not wanting her to delay with further studies. It was a constant source of tension, as Sana harbored dreams of earning a degree and carving out a path for herself.

She expressed her fears of being pushed into a life she wasn't ready for, her voice tinged with frustration and sadness. Inam listened intently, understanding the weight of her words and the conflict she was facing. He admired her determination to pursue her education and assured her that her dreams were worth fighting for.

Inam's support meant everything to Sana. He encouraged her to stand firm in her desires and not to give up on what she truly wanted, more than her brother. Knowing she had someone who believed in her, Sana felt a renewed sense of strength. With Inam by her side, she felt more confident in her ability to chase her dreams, even if it meant going against the expectations set for her.

Sana often found herself thinking about her mother's pressure and the looming possibility of an arranged marriage. In her moments of reflection, she realized that if she had to marry someone, it would be Inam. He, was the only person she felt confident, would support her dreams of continuing her studies. Sana believed that Inam would either encourage her to pursue her education or patiently wait until she completed it, understanding the importance of her goals.

Down here, Riya couldn't help but admire the way Arjun carried himself, especially when he was in the kitchen. There was something about the way he cooked, moving with confidence and ease, that captivated her. But it wasn't just his cooking skills that drew her in—it was his ability to lead, to bring everyone together with his calm and composed demeanor.

She found herself particularly impressed by how effortlessly Arjun could persuade others. Whether it was a simple suggestion or a more complex argument, Arjun had a way of making people see things from his perspective. His words carried weight, and he knew exactly how to use them to influence those around him. There was a respect and a quiet fondness that had been growing within her, sparked by the qualities she saw in him and the way he made others feel valued and understood.

On the other hand, Arjun had always seen Riya as the perfect match for him. In his eyes, she embodied everything he could ever want in a partner. Her talkative nature and rugged personality were traits he admired deeply, as they brought a lively energy to every conversation and situation they shared.

Riya's open-heartedness was another quality that Arjun cherished. She was unafraid to speak her mind and express her feelings, making her a breath of fresh air in his life. This honesty and authenticity resonated with Arjun, who found comfort in knowing that she was always genuine in her interactions with him and others.

What truly solidified Arjun's feelings was how he saw himself reflected in her. Despite their differences, there was a deep connection between them—a shared understanding and mutual respect. Arjun felt that Riya understood him in ways that others didn't, and this realization only strengthened his belief that she was the one he wanted by his side.

Later, we realized there were no drinks to serve. Rhenius, ever the dependable one, immediately stepped up and took responsibility for the situation. Without hesitation, he and Anandh decided to head into town, just 2 kilometers away, to buy some drinks for the group.

With Rhenius and Anandh gone, I decided to join Inam and Sana, sensing that they might appreciate some company. The three of us chatted easily, enjoying the lighthearted atmosphere. Meanwhile, Riya found herself happily engrossed in conversation with Arjun, the "master-chef," savoring the time she had to admire his skills and connect with him further.

As we spent time together, I naturally took on the role of a guide for Inam and Sana, showing them around my ancestral house. The place was filled with antiques and precious items, each with its own story and history. I led them through the various rooms, pointing out the unique artifacts and sharing the tales behind them. Inam and Sana seemed genuinely interested, and it felt good to share the rich heritage of the house with them, adding another layer to the evening's experience.

We began our tour at the wall near the stairs, where the portraits of my ancestors hung in a long, silent row. The paintings were old, their colors faded with time, but the eyes in each portrait seemed remarkably alive, almost as if they were watching us. As we moved, it felt like their gaze followed us wherever we went, adding an eerie yet fascinating atmosphere to the house. Inam and Sana exchanged glances, intrigued by the sense of history and mystery these portraits brought to the place.

The largest portrait of all was that of my great-great-grandfather, an antiquarian and the original owner of this majestic house. His image dominated the wall, with a presence that was hard to ignore. He had a thick, impressive mustache and a long, flowing beard, giving him a look of stern authority. As we stood before his portrait, I could see Inam and Sana taking in the details, clearly struck by the commanding figure that had once ruled over the very halls we were now exploring.

In the late 19th century, during a significant archaeological discovery, the mummy of Ramesses II was found along with those of 50 other kings and nobles. Remarkably, my great-great-grandfather managed to acquire one of these mummies—a testament to his influence and connections at the time. This relic was still kept in the house, carefully preserved in a secluded room. As I mentioned this to Inam and Sana, their eyes widened in awe, the weight of the history surrounding us becoming even more palpable.

As we continued our exploration of the house, I showed Inam and Sana another remarkable piece of history: a large Persian rug that had been passed down through generations. This rug, which once belonged to my great-great-grandfather, was truly a masterpiece. Its intricate designs were still vibrant despite its age, and the craftsmanship hinted at its origin from centuries ago. The rug had been carefully preserved, occupying a prominent place in one of the main rooms, adding to the house's air of timeless elegance.

Even as I spoke about the Persian rug, describing its intricate designs and rich history, I noticed that Sana 's attention was elsewhere. Her eyes remained fixed on the doorway leading to the room where the mummy was kept. The allure of the ancient artifact, with all its mystery and history, had clearly captured her imagination far more than anything else in the house. Despite my efforts to shift her focus, it was evident that the mummy held a fascination that she couldn't quite shake off.

Seeing how captivated Sana was by the mummy, I decided to share more about its mysterious history. I told her about a story my grandfather used to tell me—a tale that had been passed down through our family. According to him, the mummy had the potential to come to life and regain its immortality under certain conditions. It was a story that always sent shivers down my spine as a child.

I pointed out that, near the mummy, there was an old, crinkly book, covered in dust and bound in worn leather. The book was said to contain ancient rituals and secrets related to the mummy. It was another relic that had been kept in our house for generations, adding to the eerie aura that surrounded the mummy and the room where it rested.

I continued, telling Sana that my grandfather always warned me about the book. He was adamant that the book held secrets not meant for just anyone's eyes. He mentioned that a special key was needed to open it, but frustratingly, he never revealed anything more about the key—what it looked like, where it was hidden, or even if it was still in the house. It was as if he wanted to protect the mystery as much as he wanted to protect us from whatever the book contained. This only added to the book's mystique, leaving us with more questions than answers.

Meanwhile, in the kitchen, Riya and Arjun were having their own moments together. As Riya tasted the food that Arjun had prepared with Shaun's assistance, she couldn't help but be impressed. The flavors were rich and perfectly balanced, a testament to Arjun's skill in the kitchen. Riya complimented him, her admiration for him growing with every bite. Arjun, pleased with her reaction, smiled as they continued to bond over the meal, sharing laughter and light-hearted conversation.

The food was nearly finished, with Shaun adding his final touches to ensure everything was perfect. Arjun, eager to serve the meal to everyone, started preparing the dishes for the table. Before they moved on, Riya, Shaun, and Arjun couldn't resist testing the dish one last time. Shaun grabbed three pieces of chicken, offering them around for a final taste test. As they savored the bites, all three nodded in approval, satisfied that the meal was ready to impress the rest of the group.

Sana remained captivated by the mummy, still lingering in the room where it was kept, her thoughts absorbed by its ancient mystery. Meanwhile, Inam and I had moved on, finding a quiet corner to reminisce about our old times. We had always been the closest in the group, and it felt natural to slip back into the easy camaraderie we shared. Between silly jokes and teasing, I couldn't resist bringing up the day he got into trouble during our school days and ended up getting beaten by one of the staff. Inam groaned, laughing as he tried to defend himself, but we both knew it was just another fond memory that had bonded us over the years.

Later, as we were lost in our conversation, we suddenly heard Shaun's voice booming from the kitchen, "Come on, let's eat, or I'll finish it with one of my hands". "Food!" The moment we heard that magic word, Inam and I exchanged quick glances and, without a second thought, bolted down the stairs towards the dining table. The promise of a delicious meal was all the motivation we needed, and we raced to be the first ones there, eager to dig in.

Despite our eagerness, we had to hold ourselves back and wait for Rhenius and Anandh to return. They had gone to buy drinks for everyone, and it didn't feel right to start without them. So, we settled at the table, the aroma of the food making it even harder to resist, but we knew we had to be patient until the whole group was together.

A few moments later, just as we were trying to distract ourselves from the tempting smell of the food, we suddenly heard the sound of someone running. It was Sana , bursting into the room with wide eyes and a breathless voice. She came screaming, "I found it!" The urgency in her voice caught everyone's attention, and we all turned to her, curious and a bit alarmed by what she had discovered.

She whispered, "The key," in a low, almost trembling voice. My heart sank as I realized what she was talking about. Only I could fully grasp the potential disaster that could unfold if she had used that key to open the book—the very book that wasn't meant to be touched, the one kept near the Pharaoh's mummy. The gravity of the situation hit me hard, and a sense of dread crept in as I imagined the ancient secrets and possible curses that book might unleash.

I quickly asked, "Did you do anything?" My voice was sharper than I intended, fueled by the fear of what might have been unleashed. Inam immediately grew tense, clearly taken aback by my reaction. I could see him instinctively move to stand by Sana, ready to defend her, his concern for her evident. But the gravity of the situation weighed heavily on me. She might have unknowingly set events in motion that could spell disaster—not just for us, but possibly for the entire world.

Even as I grappled with the fear of what Sana might have done, the truth was, I didn't fully know the consequences myself. The stories my grandfather told were shrouded in mystery and filled with ominous warnings, but they never detailed exactly what would happen if the book was opened. The uncertainty only made the situation more terrifying. I could feel the tension in the room rising, with everyone waiting anxiously for Sana 's response, all of us caught between fear of the unknown and the hope that nothing had been set in motion.

Sana clarified that she had opened the book herself but had done nothing else, and nothing unusual had happened. Our concern over the book quickly overshadowed our earlier hunger, and we forgot about the food on the table. Driven by a mix of curiosity and anxiety, we rushed back to the room to inspect the book and ensure everything was as it should be.

When we arrived, we found the book lying open just as Sana had described. The mummy, however, was still in its place, appearing unchanged. The sight of the book and the unmoved mummy did little to ease our tension as we struggled to determine if any harm had truly been done.

I picked up the book and began reading through its pages. The text was filled with cryptic, magical words that I struggled to pronounce correctly. Initially, I didn't realize they were magical, but as I continued reading, I came across a section detailing the consequences of those words. It became clear that they were indeed imbued with magical powers, and I was struck with a sense of dread as I realized the gravity of the situation.

As I delved deeper into the book, I discovered that the magical words only took effect when spoken by a true couple or true lovers. This added a new layer of complexity to the situation, as it meant the spell or enchantment would only activate under very specific conditions, requiring genuine affection and connection between the speakers. The realization brought a mix of relief and uncertainty.

Since I was still single and none of us fit the criteria, the immediate threat seemed to be minimized. We decided to leave the book where it was and shifted our focus back to the dinner. We went downstairs, finally ready to enjoy the meal that had been prepared, letting the earlier tension give way to the comfort of good food and camaraderie.

However, Rhenius and Anandh still hadn't arrived, and only four of us were present in the hall. To our shock, Inam and Sana were missing. I knew about the affection between them, and the thought that they might have been drawn together by the book's magic left me feeling uneasy. The possibility of another heart attack loomed as I rushed to find them, my mind racing with the fear of what might have happened.

Inam and Sana approached, expressing their frustration and joking about how they weren't a true couple. While it started off as light-hearted banter, I quickly realized the gravity of the situation. My mind raced with the unsettling possibility that something more serious might have occurred between them while we were distracted. The earlier relief turned into renewed anxiety as I considered what might have happened in that room.

Inam and Sana had been excited to test the magical words themselves, eager to see if they would work. They had tried saying the words out loud, hoping to activate the magic. However, when nothing happened, they were disappointed and worried, realizing that the spell only worked for true couples. Their experiment had failed, and their concern stemmed from this failed attempt and its implications, not from any test imposed by the book.

Inam and Sana were confused and concerned about whether their failed attempt meant they weren't a true couple or if the magic in the book was simply false. The lack of any magical effect left them questioning their relationship's authenticity and the validity of the book's claims. This uncertainty only added to their frustration and worry.

Seeing their frustration, I felt a wave of relief wash over me. Their failed attempt meant that the magic words wouldn't unleash any unknown powers, and it also indicated that they didn't truly love each other in the way the spell required. However, this relief was tinged with concern as I realized the potential strain this might put on their relationship. The doubts and insecurities stirred up by this experience could lead to problems between them, and I worried about how they would navigate those challenges.

We all gathered around Inam and Sana , trying to lift their spirits. We reassured them that just because the magic didn't work now, it didn't mean their love wasn't real—it could grow stronger in the future. After some lighthearted encouragement, we convinced them to sit together and enjoy the evening without overthinking the situation.

As we finally settled down, ready for Arjun to serve the long-awaited meal, my phone rang. It was Anandh and Rhenius, calling to let us know they were just outside the house and would be arriving in about five minutes.

Suddenly, we all froze as the sound of footsteps echoed through the house. It wasn't just me this time—everyone heard it. Our eyes instinctively turned towards the stairs, where we could see a shadowy figure slowly emerging, descending towards us. The atmosphere grew tense as we tried to make out who or what it was, the earlier relief replaced by a creeping sense of unease.

The figure that emerged was gigantic, towering over us with an intimidating presence. As it descended the stairs, we could see the unmistakable features of an ancient king, his body wrapped in mummified threads that clung to his form like a shroud. The sight was surreal and terrifying, the once-distant stories of the mummy suddenly brought to life before our very eyes. Every step it took echoed ominously, filling the room with a dread that was almost palpable.

As the terrifying figure approached, the fear in the room was nearly overwhelming. But then, to everyone's surprise, I noticed two of us smiling—Inam and Sana . They exchanged a look, clearly amused, as if this strange occurrence somehow validated their relationship. They seemed to believe that their love was true after all, and that this was proof. The rest of us were stunned by their reaction, caught between the fear of the looming figure and the shock of Inam and Sana 's unexpected calmness and amusement.

As the mummy came closer, we realized he wasn't as menacing as we had feared. His eyes, instead of being dark and hollow, glowed softly with a light that seemed almost gentle. The initial terror we felt began to shift into a strange mix of curiosity and confusion. This ancient king, once feared in the tales passed down through generations, stood before us not as a malevolent force, but as something else entirely. The light in his eyes hinted at a presence that was more than just a terrifying relic of the past.

The mummy finally spoke, his voice deep and ancient, resonating through the room. "It's good to be back," he said, his glowing eyes scanning the room, taking in our shocked expressions. "I can feel it—my immortality will be restored soon." His words sent a chill down my spine, turning our confusion into a new wave of fear. The reality of what we had unleashed began to sink in, and the gravity of the situation became terrifyingly clear.

Just as the weight of the mummy's words began to settle in, we heard a familiar, slightly sarcastic voice break the tension. "It's good for you, but for us..." Shaun said, his tone carrying that unique blend of humor and exasperation. The contrast between the mummy's ominous declaration and Shaun's quip was almost surreal, and despite the fear, a nervous chuckle escaped some of us. Shaun's comment, while laced with nervousness, somehow lightened the moment, reminding us that even in the strangest situations, he could still find a way to bring some levity.

The mummy responded to Shaun's quip with a low, gently evil laugh that sent a shiver through the room. "It will be fine for you," he said, his voice both calming and menacing, "if you all stand by my side." We exchanged uneasy glances, realizing that whatever this ancient being had in mind, it involved us, and the choice he presented felt like a dangerous crossroads. The tension in the room thickened as we tried to process what he was asking of us and what it would mean to align ourselves with him.

Arjun's voice broke the tense silence, but instead of sounding bold, it was laced with a mix of fear and forced humor. "It's our house, bro," he said, trying to keep his tone light but clearly nervous. "Ask him to leave, go back to his mortal state, or whatever." The attempt at humor was evident, but so was the underlying fear in his voice. His words, though meant to be funny, added a strange layer of irony to the situation. The rest of us, caught between anxiety and the absurdity of Arjun's remark, didn't know whether to laugh or panic as we braced for the mummy's reaction.

As the tension in the room mounted, everyone suddenly turned to me. I was standing at the front, closest to the mummy. They all looked at me expectantly, and with a mix of nervousness and forced humor, they said, "It's your ancestors' house, boy, so you negotiate with him." The responsibility of dealing with this ancient being was suddenly thrust upon me, and I could feel the weight of their gazes, half-serious and half-pleading, as I stood there, trying to figure out how to respond to the situation that had spiraled so wildly out of control.

I stood there, feeling the weight of the moment as I stared directly at the mummy. Summoning whatever courage I could muster, I asked politely, "So, what is your plan now that you've returned to the mortal world?" My voice was steady, but the nervous energy in the room was palpable. I hoped that engaging him in conversation might buy us some time—or at least give us some insight into what he intended to do next.

The mummy responded in a way none of us expected. "I've just come back, dude," he said, almost casually, with an unusual tone of pleading in his ancient voice. "Give me some time." The odd mix of his ancient presence and modern slang was so bizarre it caught us all off guard. It was as if this once-terrifying figure was now just another person trying to figure things out. The tension in the room shifted, and I wasn't sure whether to be more confused or relieved by his unexpected response.

Surprised by the mummy's casual use of modern slang, I couldn't help but ask, "How can you speak like that?" His response caught us all completely off guard. With a smirk, he revealed, "Well, no one expected that mummification would preserve more than just my body. Turns out, I've been listening in on the living for a long time, picking up on your language, your habits... everything."

His words sent a chill through the room. The realization that this ancient being had been silently observing the modern world for who knows how long was both fascinating and unsettling. None of us had anticipated this twist, and the room fell into a stunned silence as we processed what he had just revealed.

I asked, trying to regain my composure, "So, when will you receive your gift of immortality?" The question hung in the air, charged with a mix of curiosity and apprehension. The mummy's response would likely reveal not only his immediate plans but also what this supposed immortality entailed for us and the rest of the world.

The mummy's eyes glinted as he scanned the room. "I can sense some food here," he said, his tone shifting to one of interest. It was clear he was intrigued by the scent of the meal we had prepared. His focus seemed to momentarily shift from immortality to the prospect of food, adding a strange twist to the situation.

The mummy, now clearly interested in the food, extended an unexpected invitation. "Join me in the feast you had planned for yourselves," he said, his tone surprisingly courteous. Despite the strange and unsettling circumstances, it seemed he wanted to partake in the meal we had prepared. We exchanged glances, unsure whether to accept his invitation or refuse, but the idea of sharing our meal with this ancient being added an even more bizarre twist to our evening.

As Arjun began serving the Pharaoh, we were jolted by the sudden sound of the doorbell. The tension in the room spiked, and we exchanged nervous glances, wondering what could possibly happen next. Gathering what little courage we had left, we opened the door to find Rhenius and Anandh standing there, their faces reflecting a mix of confusion and shock.

They were stunned to see us all gathered around the dining table with the ancient Pharaoh, whom they initially mistook for an "old man." The bizarre sight left them speechless, as they struggled to comprehend how we had gone from a simple dinner to sharing a meal with a mummified king from the past.

Rhenius and Anandh approached me, their faces filled with bewilderment. They whispered in my ear, "What's going on? Who's he in the mummy costume?" Their ignorance about the true nature of the situation was evident, as they struggled to grasp whether the Pharaoh was merely someone in costume or something far more extraordinary.

As the food was served and the Pharaoh reached out to take his portion, I stopped him. With a mix of urgency and curiosity, I asked again, "When will you receive the gift of immortality?" The question lingered in the air, the tension in the room heightening as we awaited his response.

As the food was served and the Pharaoh reached out to take his portion, I stopped him. With a mix of urgency and curiosity, I asked again, "When will you receive the gift of immortality?" The question lingered in the air, the tension in the room heightening as we awaited his response. The Pharaoh looked up from the food and answered, "I need my wife to arrive."

Arjun, trying to make sense of the situation, suggested, "Maybe he doesn't like our recipe and needs his own to make the food." Shaun, shaking his head, countered, "He hasn't even touched our food, man." Shaun, clearly on edge, added with frustration, "I'm already frightened, and now you're making me more nervous. Just shut your mouth, bro." His exasperation highlighted the growing tension and fear among us, as we struggled to navigate the bizarre and unsettling situation with the Pharaoh.

The Pharaoh explained, "To gain my gift of immortality, my wife must arrive." His statement clarified that the completion of his immortality was contingent on the presence of his wife. This new revelation added a crucial element to the unfolding situation, as we now faced the challenge of understanding and possibly facilitating the arrival of this significant figure.

We realized that the Pharaoh would remain mortal until his wife arrived. His immortality was contingent on her presence, and until then, he was just like any other human. This understanding added a new layer to our situation, as we now had to figure out how to either facilitate her arrival or address the consequences of her absence.

I pressed the Pharaoh with a smirk, "When will she be coming?" while playfully keeping him from touching the dish. My attempt to make light of the situation seemed to add an element of humor to the tension, as I used the moment to poke fun at the Pharaoh's predicament while we waited for more answers.

The Pharaoh, growing increasingly frustrated, said, "What do you want, bro? You're not even letting me touch the food." His irritation was clear as he struggled with the delay and the situation's absurdity, making it evident that he was eager to move past the interruptions and enjoy the meal.

We couldn't help but giggle at his frustration, but before we could react, the Pharaoh quickly moved and grabbed some food, determined not to be thwarted again. His swift action caught us off guard, and the room erupted in a mix of nervous laughter and disbelief as the ancient king finally got his hands on the meal.

After the laughter subsided, I gently asked him, "Why do you need your wife to gain your immortality?" My curiosity got the better of me, and I wanted to understand the significance of her presence in his quest for eternal life. The room grew quiet as we all awaited his explanation, eager to uncover more of the mystery surrounding this ancient figure.

After finishing his first bite of food, the Pharaoh looked at me thoughtfully. The room was still as we all waited for his response, hoping to finally understand why his wife's presence was so crucial to his immortality.

The Pharaoh paused, then asked, "What was the food I was eating?" His curiosity caught us off guard, and we quickly realized he had never tasted anything like our modern dishes before. It was a strange moment, mixing ancient mystique with something as simple as a meal.

As soon as we told him it was tomato rice and chicken, he quickly responded, "My wife has to be here because our immortality was a gift given to us because of our love." His immediate reply left no room for hesitation, revealing the deep connection between their love and the power they were meant to share. The sudden clarity in his words added a sense of urgency to the situation, making it clear that their bond was the key to everything.

His response was quick, but there was a noticeable edge of anger in his voice. As he spoke, we noticed his eyes starting to change, a subtle shift in their color and intensity. The atmosphere in the room grew tense as his demeanor shifted, signalling that this was more than just a casual conversation—something powerful and potentially dangerous was stirring within him.

As the Pharaoh's anger simmered, the lights in the room began to flicker erratically, casting unsettling shadows around us. Suddenly, the television turned on by itself, filling the room with static before settling on a news broadcast. The abruptness of it all heightened the tension, as if something was building up, ready to break loose.

The news headline was even more disturbing. It reported that a storm had formed directly over our location. The storm was described as small in radius but incredibly powerful. This ominous coincidence made it feel as though the storm was connected to the Pharaoh's rising emotions, intensifying the unease that was already gripping us. It was as if the forces of nature were responding to the ancient king's anger, adding a new layer of dread to the situation.

Everything stopped suddenly—the lights stabilized, the television went silent, and the eerie flickering ceased. The tension that had gripped the room dissipated as quickly as it had come. We cautiously turned our attention back to the news, only to see that the storm, which had appeared so ominous moments ago, was now gone without a trace. It was as if the entire episode had been nothing more than a strange, fleeting moment of chaos.

As we took a breath of relief, we noticed something shocking—our entire place was almost completely covered in sand. The storm may have vanished, but it had left behind a surreal landscape, as if we had been transported to a desert. Sand filled the corners of the room, spilling in through windows and doors, covering the floors, and burying everything in a thick layer. The once familiar surroundings now felt foreign and eerie, as if the storm had brought a piece of the ancient world into our modern lives.

Just as we were trying to process the scene, something even stranger occurred. The particles of sand began to stir, gathering together in the center of the room. We watched in disbelief as the sand started to swirl, forming a small, concentrated whirlwind right inside our house. The swirl of wind grew stronger, whipping the sand into a tight vortex, as if something—or someone—was trying to take shape within it. The surreal spectacle left us frozen in place, unsure of what was about to happen next.

As the sand vortex intensified, it suddenly dispersed, revealing a stunningly beautiful woman standing where the swirl had been. Her appearance was otherworldly, with features that spoke of a time long past. Draped in ancient, regal attire, she exuded an aura of elegance and power. The room fell silent as she turned her gaze toward the Pharaoh, her expression gentle and filled with a deep, timeless connection. It was clear that she was his long-awaited wife, the key to his immortality.

The revelation of the woman's arrival was terrifying in its implications. She wasn't there simply to reunite with her husband but had been summoned by his anger—a curse from ancient times. Her purpose was far more sinister: to destroy those who had dared to provoke the Pharaoh's wrath.

As she moved closer to him, her gentle expression shifted into something more menacing, and we realized with horror what was about to unfold. The air grew thick with tension as the Pharaoh's anger, which had seemed to dissipate, now began to pulse again with renewed intensity. The curse had been triggered, and we were its targets.

Panic set in as we realized we had to act quickly. We had inadvertently unleashed an ancient force, and now our only hope was to find a way to appease the Pharaoh and his wife before it was too late. We might try to reason with them, offer an apology, or even reverse the magic somehow. The room, once filled with curiosity and wonder, was now a battleground for survival against the fury of a couple cursed to destroy those who wronged them.

As the tension escalated, everyone's eyes turned to me. They all pointed in my direction, silently urging me to step forward and negotiate with the woman who now threatened us all. My heart pounded in my chest as I realized that our lives were hanging in the balance.

I hesitated for a moment, feeling the weight of responsibility on my shoulders. But there was no time to waste—the Pharaoh's wife, with her ominous presence, was ready to carry out the curse. Taking a deep breath, I stepped forward, trying to project confidence despite the fear gripping me.

Her eyes flared with a dark intensity as she shouted in an ominous, echoing voice, "Our era rises again! No one can stop us!" The room shook with the power of her words, and a chilling sense of dread washed over us all.

It was clear that her mind was set—this was no mere warning, but a declaration of their intent to reclaim their lost power and bring forth the resurgence of an ancient era. The shadows in the room seemed to grow darker, the air colder, as if the very atmosphere was bending to her will.

In a desperate attempt to reason with them, I boldly spoke up, "We are the ones who set you free, allowing you to finally attain your immortality. If it weren't for us, you would still be trapped, your power locked away for eternity. Please, leave us in peace as a token of gratitude for our unwitting help."

The room fell silent as my words hung in the air. The Pharaoh and his wife exchanged glances, their ancient eyes reflecting a mix of thoughts. For a moment, it seemed like they were considering my plea. The tension was unbearable as we waited for their response, hoping that this appeal to their sense of honor—or at least to their desire for freedom—might be enough to spare us from their wrath.

The Pharaoh and his wife ignored my plea, their faces revealing nothing as they turned to each other, speaking in low, ominous tones. "We need a palace," the wife said, her voice dripping with ancient authority. The Pharaoh's gaze swept across the room, and a cold realization settled in as he replied, "This ancestral house—it will serve our purpose."

The house, my family's home for generations, was now their target. They saw it as the perfect place to reestablish their dominion, a new seat of power for their resurrection. We were no longer just dealing with an ancient curse but were now facing the loss of everything—the house, our lives, and the world as we knew it.

The situation had escalated beyond our control, and it was clear that reasoning with them was no longer an option. We needed to act, and fast, if we were to stop them from claiming my ancestral home as their new palace and prevent the return of an era long buried in history.

In the midst of the tension, someone from our group blurted out, "It's our house, you dead immortal king guy!" The words hung in the air, a defiant challenge to the Pharaoh's claim. But instead of reacting with immediate anger, the Pharaoh paused, his lips curling into a faint, cold smile. It was clear that while he was amused by our bravery, he wasn't going to let it deter him from his plan.

Arjun, never one to back down, stepped forward with a calm but firm voice. "You stay on the other side, and we'll stay on this side," he declared, drawing an invisible line between us and the ancient couple. Arjun stepped forward and suggested, "We could share our kitchen." His proposal aimed to find a compromise and ease the tension between us and the Pharaoh. The room fell silent as we awaited the Pharaoh's reaction, hoping that this offer might lead to a peaceful resolution.

The Pharaoh gave the food that we had already served him a scrutinizing look. He seemed to evaluate it with an air of ancient judgment, as if determining whether it met the standards of his long-forgotten tastes. Suddenly, the Pharaoh and his wife said, "Okay." No one was expecting this sudden change. The unexpected agreement left everyone in the room momentarily stunned, as they processed the abrupt shift in their demands.

I had to take on the role of guide once more, but this time it was for the immortal couple, not my friends. Arjun stepped in to help, and together we navigated them through the house, carefully outlining their boundaries and trying to ensure that their presence didn't escalate the already tense situation.

So, there was this hall where the couple tended to stay. It was a grand space, with high ceilings and ornate decorations that seemed to suit their ancient and regal presence. We left them in the hall to enjoy their own modern time, hoping it would keep them occupied. Meanwhile, we focused on finding a way to prevent their destruction and protect our home.

We were still starving, having waited too long while dealing with the unexpected situation. The meal we had prepared earlier now seemed like a distant memory as we tried to figure out how to resolve the crisis. Shaun, Arjun, Riya, Inam, and Sana finally sat down to have their meal. Despite the earlier chaos, they were relieved to finally enjoy the food and take a moment to unwind.

In the meantime, Anandh, Rhenius, and I went upstairs to the room where we first saw the Egyptian dead king. We hoped to gather more information or find something that might help us deal with the situation. There, the book was covered with sand, a result of the recent storm. It was partially buried, its ancient pages barely visible under the layer of debris.

When I tried to touch the book, it wouldn't let me. An unseen force seemed to prevent my hand from making contact, as if the book itself was resisting any attempt to move it. A sudden thought came to my mind: "love." I wondered if it might be the key to overcoming whatever barrier was preventing me from touching the book.

I went rushing down the stairs, driven by the sudden thought that "love" might be the solution. My urgency was fueled by the hope that this insight could provide a way to address the mysterious force keeping us from the book.

I went to call Inam and Sana, as their love had the power to break the curse. I hoped that their presence would help us lift the barrier preventing us from touching the book.

Now that Inam and Sana opened the book, something remarkable happened. As they flipped through its ancient pages, only they could see the words inscribed within. The text, hidden from the rest of us, seemed to be written specifically for them.

Inam and Sana began reading the words aloud, their voices steady as they recited the ancient script. As they spoke, the air around us felt charged with an unfamiliar energy, almost as if the words themselves carried a power we couldn't fully comprehend. We all listened intently, hoping these words would bring the answers we needed.

As Inam and Sana finished reading, the book revealed a final passage. It stated that the pharaohs, though they had been granted immortality, could return to their eternal rest if they so wished. The choice was theirs—to remain in the mortal world or return to the afterlife they had once left behind. This revelation left us all silent, realizing that their fate was now in their hands.

We retreated to our side of the house, leaving the immortal couple to their thoughts. Gathering in the dining area, we brainstormed, trying to figure out how to convince the pharaoh and his queen to return to their eternal rest. The atmosphere was tense, we needed a plan, and fast, before things got out of hand.

Suddenly, Inam and Sana started arguing, their voices rising above the already tense atmosphere. The fight seemed to come out of nowhere, but it quickly escalated, with each word cutting deeper. The rest of us exchanged worried glances, unsure if this was just stress or something more ominous. Their disagreement was the last thing we needed at that moment.

As Inam and Sana 's argument heated up, a piercing scream echoed through the house, freezing everyone in place. It was the queen, her voice filled with pain and anguish. The sound was so intense that it sent chills down our spines, making us wonder what had just happened and whether it was connected to the tension brewing among us.

The queen and the Pharaoh descended quickly, their expressions a mix of concern and urgency. In a surprisingly gentle tone, they asked where the young couple—Inam and Sana —was. The shift in their demeanour was striking, as if they had been deeply affected by the recent events and were now seeking the couple for a reason we didn't yet understand.

The queen and Pharaoh began to inquire about the source of the conflict between Imam and Sana. After hearing us out, they gently suggested that Inam and Sana should stay united and support each other. The pharaoh and queen emphasised the importance of their bond, believing that it was crucial for overcoming the challenges they faced.

The queen and Pharaoh began to share their own love story, starting with a memory from their teenage years.

"The queen and Pharaoh recounted how they first met in the market when they were teenagers. The young Pharaoh was immediately captivated by the queen's beauty and grace. Their relationship blossomed from that moment, with their love growing stronger despite the complexities of their shared heritage.

The young Pharaoh, struck by the queen's beauty, sought to learn more about her. He asked his nobles for information and discovered that she was, in fact, his relative. This revelation only intensified his feelings for her, as their shared lineage added a layer of destiny to their burgeoning romance.

The young Pharaoh began visiting the market frequently, eager to catch glimpses of the queen. His regular visits were driven by his desire to see her and deepen their connection, despite the constraints of their social positions. Each encounter in the bustling marketplace strengthened his affection and commitment to her.

By the age of 16, their feelings had grown so strong that they began considering marriage. They saw a future together, envisioning a life united despite the obstacles they might face. Their young love was filled with hope and determination, reflecting their deep commitment to one another.

However, the Pharaoh faced his first major obstacle when his mother insisted that he marry his sister, in line with their tradition of sibling marriage. This cultural expectation created a significant challenge for the young Pharaoh, putting his love for the queen to the test and marking the beginning of their struggles to be together.

Despite his mother's insistence, the Pharaoh chose to disobey her and follow his heart. His sister, understanding his deep affection for the queen, supported his decision. This act of defiance was a pivotal moment, reflecting his commitment to his love and the strength of their bond.

The Pharaoh's friends rallied behind him, offering their support and helping him navigate the challenges of his decision. They facilitated his secret meetings with the queen in the market, ensuring that their love could continue to flourish despite the obstacles they faced.

As his mother's opposition intensified, she gathered several elders from their family to intervene and halt the Pharaoh's plans. The elders were summoned to reinforce the traditional expectations and pressure him to conform to his mother's wishes, further complicating the young Pharaoh's efforts to be with the queen.

His mother insisted that he marry his sister first, suggesting that he could still marry the queen afterward, as he was allowed multiple wives. This solution was meant to uphold tradition while still providing a path for him to be with the queen in the future.

However, the Pharaoh firmly believed in the principle of having one true love. He was determined that the queen would be his one and only, rejecting the idea of marrying multiple wives as a compromise. His unwavering commitment to her was a testament to the depth of his feelings.

Enraged by his defiance, his mother and the elders took drastic measures. They forcibly sent the Pharaoh and the queen into exile, abandoning them in the forest. As they were chased away, the Pharaoh and the queen were brutally beaten. Their escape into the forest was marked by violence, intended to punish them for defying tradition and to ensure that their love would not threaten the established order.

In the forest, as their situation grew increasingly dire, the Pharaoh and the queen encountered a prophet. Just before their lives were in imminent danger, the prophet appeared. The prophet, seeing their unwavering love and suffering, bestowed upon them the gift of immortality. He explained that their sacrifice for love had earned them this eternal reward. He told them that they would be broken into the world again by a true couple, and in time, they would reclaim their rightful place.

The prophet warned that if the true lovers who broke the curse ever divorced, the Pharaoh and the queen would return to their dead state. Their immortality was thus intricately linked to the continued union of the couple who had freed them. The Pharaoh and the queen continued, "We wanted to live here, but if we ruled over humans, they might manipulate you into divorcing, which would force us to return to our dead state." They realized that their desire to stay could endanger the true couple's relationship."

The Pharaoh and the queen concluded, "Since we couldn't live together in our own time and don't want to cause you any suffering, we have decided to leave." They chose to depart, recognizing that staying could harm the true couple and disrupt their chance at happiness. The Pharaoh said that the lovers had to close the door of the room and the box where he had been placed because he had decided to return from this world.

Finally, before they returned, I asked, "From where did the queen come? We saw you here in this house, but not her." I asked, "What made her come?"

The Pharaoh explained that his anger had caused the queen to appear. We then went upstairs to the room and were about to close the door when I asked, "What made you angry?" He replied, "FOOD," just as the door closed behind us.

CHAPTER THREE

Hand in Hand

-By Aramvalarthasivagami. R

It was a chill morning. People wore three-layered clothes to warm themselves, and in houses, parents and relatives gave red pockets to children. The trees, adorned with poppy reds and tangerine oranges, brought happiness. The college students returned to their hometowns to enjoy the holidays with their families. The young children were excited to watch the fireworks in the evening.

A girl with curly brown hair and chubby cheeks was bustling around the area, handling busy work calls. She might be on a break, but she still needed to work on calls. Finally, she found some time to tidy her home. Her room was a wreck, with perfume bottles and files scattered everywhere. Before she began cleaning, she took a deep breath. After two hours of cleaning, she felt a wave of relaxation come over her, then she carried two trash bags downstairs from her apartment to throw them in the common trash can. After that, she went back to her apartment, took off her shoes, and slipped on her comfy grey bunny house slippers.

While she was packing dresses, her phone rang, then she answered her phone and greeted with "ni hao" a bit tiredly. Her mom couldn't hear her well and repeated her name, Tangcan, several times. Finally, Tangcan confirmed she could hear her. She slid the balcony glass door and stepped outside. During the call, Tangcan's mom, Zhou Ran, mentioned that Aunt Vivian would pick up Tang at the Hexi bus stop. Tang replied, "I can walk there by myself, Mom; don't worry." Then Zhou reminded her to get Vivian Sung's favorite perfume, Tom Ford Black Orchid, and for her, Brown Homie, as it was her favourite. Zhou Ran asked Tangcan about what she should prepare for dinner. Tangcan said she'd be coming home tomorrow night before ending the call. Tangcan has worked in ''ZAC Perfume'' as a fragrance evaluator. Every day she wore a new perfume to get to know which one attracted the people more. In her office, the people knew her as a strict person.

She stayed with her parents until she joined a job. After that, she rented a flat near her office. Every holiday, she never missed going home to have dinner with her parents. During the spring holiday, she stayed at her aunt's house in Hexi.

On this special day, instead of enjoying the holiday for the spring festival, Tang worked tirelessly through calls until this morning. She has decided to offer discounts on the newly arrived perfumes for the Spring Festival and suggested this in the previous week's company meetings too. She took her Doraemon trolley and her costly pastel green handbag. Before reaching the bus stop, she went to a convenience store to buy tea. Tang walked towards the convenience store. At the entrance, the glass doors opened automatically, allowing her to enter. It was a small store, with just four columns and three rows of shelves. The first two columns of the first row were stocked with food items, while the last two columns held vegetables and fruits. In the second row, the first two columns were filled with beauty products, and the last two columns displayed detergent, spices, garam masala, and oils. The entire last row was dedicated to household items and stationery. Tang turned to her right and passed the billing counter, then turned right again. At the end of the first row, she found a refrigerator full of drinks and ice creams. She bought bubble tea and soy milk. She paid the yuan at the billing counter. Then she put them into her bag.

Now she was ready to take the bus to Hexi, where she had spent her childhood days. The bus arrived; it was a white bus with windows covering half the height of its sides. The door opened automatically. She entered the bus, where the driver was seated on the left side. On the right side was a card reader and smart ticket validator machine that passengers used to pay for their tickets. After paying money through WeChat to pay for the ticket, the bus started. It was a celebration day, so the bus was not crowded. She moved toward an empty seat and sat by the window, then put wired headphones in her ears. The cool breeze, along with her memories, made her feel more cherished. Suddenly, her music stopped, and her phone rang with the sound of a frog ringtone. With a gracious smile, she greeted her aunt, Vivian Sung, with "Happy Spring Festival." Vivian asked Tangcan where she was. Tangcan replied that she had just crossed Nankai and would arrive in about two hours, then Vivian asked, "Did you have your breakfast?" Tang replied, "Yes, I did." Then she said, "Okay, let me know once you reach Hexi," and she ended the call.

Tang's eyes were shining with happiness; her body was just moving by breathing. All her mind ran her happy memories of her childhood in Hexi. She repeatedly looks at her watch with a little tension about when she will reach Hexi. She took her phone to pass the time; she opened WeChat to reply to the unread messages. After replying to all the Chinese New Year wishes, she put her iPhone inside her cozy handbag.

The bus stopped at the Heping bus stop. A lady with brown eyes got into the bus with her five-year-old child. That boy ran towards an empty seat near Tangcan; his mom said, "Steven, don't run in the bus." Tangcan turned aside and smiled at that boy with excitement. She grabbed his hand and made him sit next to her. Steven's mom got a seat back to him.

Steven glanced at her with a hint of confusion. Tangcan took a Hershey's chocolate to Steven; he silently turned back and looked at his mom with sympathy. After his mom smiled, he happily grabbed that chocolate from Tangcan. Still, she has an hour to reach Hexi. So, she decided to engage him in a game; subsequently took her phone and started playing with her crazy juicer.

Steven's stomach growled loudly, and Tang's eyes sparkled with understanding. She smiled warmly and took a bubble tea and soy milk from her bag. As she offered him the soy milk, his mom said, "Steven is allergic to soy milk, dear." Tang's face fell, and she quietly handed him the bubble tea instead. Tang felt a deep connection with Steven. She turned back to the window and was lost in thoughts, a single tear escaped her left eye, glistening in the light.

In the park, children were running all around the ground and playing with their friends. "A little boy with a partially raised right arm, his hand waving up and down and calling his friend, his pal running in front of him, she slightly turned her face with a playful smile. Suddenly, two hands seized that little girl's arms, her eyes widened in shock as the darkness closed in, warping her in an inky blackness that seemed to suffocate her, snapping her back to the present. Tang's face was drenched in sweat as she snapped back to reality. Steven's voice echoed in her ears, "Bye-bye, Miss Tang,"" as she jerked awake, realizing she had reached her stop at Hexi and needed to step off the bus. She took her trolley and handbag and then stepped off the bus.

From the bus stop to Vivian Sung's apartment, there is a distance of two kilometers. Tang's aunt has a Volkswagen Passat car and said she would pick up Tang. Tang expressed her desire to revisit her memories of the place by mentioning that she would come on her own. The cool breeze gave a warm welcome. She grabbed her Doraemon trolley and started to walk. She crossed the road and took the left direction; there the road separated into two; she took again left; her heart snapped the directions.

It was mid-afternoon, and the streets were quiet, with few people around. White oak trees shed their leaves, which gently fell around her. She placed her handbag on the trolley's grip handle and enjoyed the feel of the leaves brushing against her right palm. Suddenly, her expression shifted as a familiar smell filled the air. Her nose caught the aroma, and her feet instinctively followed its source. It led her to a small food shop called "Dreamy Dumplings." She paused, her eyes widening with recognition. The elderly man who ran the shop was busy serving a handful of customers. Tang's heart swelled with happiness. This was a place from her childhood, a place full of cherished memories. She recalled the old version of the dumpling shop in her mind, remembering how the grandpa would hang a board with the day's specials on the door. The shop might have been small, but he knew how to attract customers. He would open the window to let the enticing aroma drift out, drawing people in. He often offered discounts to school students, always aiming to make them happy. He prioritised using healthy ingredients in his cooking, and the walls were covered with cartoon pictures to capture the attention of children.

The grandpa stepped outside to answer a call, but his phone turned off due to a dead battery. He looked up and saw Tang, greeting her with a gesture of half-bending his body. Tang smiled and called out, "DD Grandpa!" The old man adjusted his spectacles, his eyes widening with joy. "How are you, Cancan?" he asked warmly. "I'm happy and doing well, DD Grandpa," she replied. He gently took her hand and led her to a small table for two. Tang looked around and said, "Grandpa, your shop has changed so much! I remember when there were only a few seats, and most people would just take their food to go. Now it looks so cool and spacious." He smiled at her, then quietly stepped away. Tang admired the new ambiance of the shop; the walls were freshly painted white and covered with hand-drawn trendy cartoons. Her eyes lit up when she spotted a drawing of Doraemon with Dorayaki. The shiny wooden tables and artifacts on the wall fetched the shop to the next level; even the menu card seemed cool with affordable prices, and the little plants on the window side looked refreshing. Just then, a familiar aroma caught her attention. DD Grandpa returned with a plate of sweet corn cheese dumplings and spicy sausage, her childhood favourite from the shop. "I didn't put this on the menu," he said with a warm smile, "but I made it especially for you." Her heart soared with joy at his words.

She was speechless as she savored every bite of the dumplings, licking her fingers clean to show just how delicious the food was. After finishing, she asked, "Grandpa, why didn't you mention you were reopening the dumpling shop when we met last year?"

Grandpa sighed and replied, "At that time, I hadn't planned on reopening. As you know, the past seven years have been tough for me. I wasn't sure if I could do it again. But two months ago, I couldn't stand seeing this place empty anymore. So, I have decided to bring it back to life with a business loan." With a smile, she said, "This shop feels like a New Year's gift to me." Tang glanced at her watch and realized it was time to leave. Grandpa noticed and said, "Looks like you have to meet someone, Tang. Come by whenever you have the time; take these parcels as a present." Tang smiled and gratefully accepted the dumpling parcels, a New Year's gift from DD Grandpa.

Rushing with her luggage, she was almost at the apartment when she noticed a little girl on a four-wheeled pink bicycle, being guided by her brother. Suddenly, a voice broke through the quiet of Tang's thoughts. "Tang, that's my cycle! You don't even know how to pedal it! Tang, stop! Stop it, Tang!" The little girl tried to brake, but she toppled over, tears welling up. Her brother hurried to help her up, while Tang quickly grabbed the bicycle and set it upright. She picked up her luggage and walked toward the children's park. The area was eerily quiet, with trees and playground slides.

Leaves gently drifted down, settling on the empty chairs, swings, and spring riders in the playground. In the park, the first square except for the gateway is covered with some trees. The second square is a pathway for walking, and the third square is arranged with flower pots, except for the four corners that lead into the children's playground. There are some wooden benches along the pathways for sitting.

Gal Cypress and Sang Yan entwined their hands, swaying in the gentle evening air. When she saw Sang Yan, her fingers loosened, and the luggage slipped from her grasp, crashing to the ground. She ran towards him, wrapping her arms around him as best as she could, though as he was chubby and strong it made it difficult. Her emotions overflowed with tears of relief mixed with a smile, expressing the depth of her feelings. The Gal seemed a bit possessive of Sang Yan, glaring furiously at Tang. As Tang loosened her arms on Sang Yan, her arms got some imprints from his body. With teary eyes, she stepped back, picked up her luggage, and slowly walked away. She kept glancing back at Sang Yan, her gaze lingering on him until she finally left the park.

Gal slightly turned away from Sang Yan, back to him. He stood there, caught in a swirl of confusion, unsure of how to comfort her. Gal spontaneously asked questions to Sang without a gasp, like "Who is she? Why did she hug you? I have been with you for the past year; I didn't even see her here; then how can she do this?" with a rough voice. Sang, with a slightly tense smile, said, "Wait, wait, I'll explain everything about her. Her name is Tangcan. Fourteen years ago, she lived here. From birth until third grade, she spent her childhood in this "New Hexi" apartment. Every Chinese New Year, she would come back to see me." As children slowly made their way into the park, chatting excitedly about the upcoming night fireworks, a heavy silence fell between Gal and Sang. Neither spoke until the children had passed by, their voices fading into the distance.

Gal, her voice tinged with possessiveness, demanded, "I'm not asking who she is. I'm asking, what's going on between you two?" Sang replied, "Let me explain." It's not just about Tang and me—it's about Steven, Tang, and me.

Tangcan's father was the editor of a popular anime comic here in Hexi. She was the only child in her family, and they lived in flat thirty-three, right next to Steven in thirty-four. Tangcan and Steven were inseparable, born in the same year and month of August, though on different days. From first grade through third, they attended the same school and were always in the same class. Steven was always by Tang's side. Back then, Tangcan was the only girl among the neighborhood children, so she was adored by all the neighbors except for the boy children, who refused to let her join in their games. Whenever TangCan asked to join their games, boys would swiftly refuse her. But Steven was always there to lift her happiness. He would take her hand and run to play, their laughter echoing in the air.

Whenever she felt down, he'd tickle her until her sadness turned into giggles. Day after day, they walked to and from school hand in hand, their bond as natural as the changing seasons.

The boys often teased Steven for always being with Tang, unlike them. But he ignored their bullying and played with her happily. Whenever Tang felt low, just seeing Steven's face and spending time with him was enough to cheer her up. It was the Spring Festival of the early 2000s, and the children were eagerly waiting to watch the Chinese New Year fireworks from the beginning of the holidays. But that spring festival holiday began in the evening, and Tangcan's father returned home with a heavy heart. He opened the door and changed the slippers; he didn't even say he came home to his wife. After his wife noticed he had come back, she gave water to him. He got the glass of water from her and put it on the table without having a sip. He sadly told his wife, Zhou Ran, that he had been transferred to a higher-paying position as the head anime editor in Nankai. However, the trip would take him four hours each day. Zhou Ran gently reassured him, saying, "You're what matters the most to us. If need be, we can move our lives to Nankai once you join there."

Tang's dad watched Tang ride Steven's bike with him from the window. As Steven partially raised his hand to stop her, he realized she didn't even know how to ride it while seeing a wistful smile on her dad's face. He sighed deeply and headed to the kitchen for a glass of herb water. Just as he raised the glass to his lips, his phone rang with the familiar default ringtone. He got irritated; he murmured under his breath, "Can't even drink a glass of water in peace," as he reluctantly grabbed the phone. It was a call from his boss. Tang Xuan picked up the phone and greeted his boss. His boss replied, "Sorry to bother you, Mr. Tang Xuan." "It's alright, sir," Xuan responded. "Is there something urgent?" His boss continued, "Actually, Xuan, the head editor at our Nankai office, had an unfortunate accident. We need you to step in, and we want you to take over as soon as the spring festival is over. You'll need to start right after the holidays. Don't worry, the company will assist with moving your things the day after New Year's, and we've already arranged a flat for you close to the Nankai office."

Xuan was stunned; the news hit him hard. He was left speechless, a mix of emotions flooding over him. He had thought there would be more time to prepare for such a big change, but now he realized the clock was ticking. The idea of relocating so soon overwhelmed him, and he wasn't sure how to break the news to his family. A soft thud came from the door, and Zhou Ran opened the door. Tang quietly stepped inside, and Zhou Ran let her inside with a warm smile. Tang gestures for silence, putting a finger to her lips. Her mother nodded, and Tang tiptoed as quietly as possible across the room. She half bent her knees and playfully raised her arms like dinosaur claws, sneaking up behind her dad with a mischievous "boo!" But her dad, lost in deep thought, gave no reaction. Tang paused, confused by his lack of response, and slowly made her way to her room, a look of confusion remaining on her face.

The next morning, Zhou Ran placed breakfast on the dining table and called Tang Can and Tang Xuan to eat. Tang Can was excited when she saw her mom had made her favorite food. Xuan, on the other hand, struggled to act normal after hearing about his sudden transfer to Nankai. As Tang Can ate rushingly, her mom reminded her, "Eat slowly and don't make a mess." In the middle of breakfast, she heard Steven's voice from outside. Even though the door was already open, Steven knocked loudly and said, "Can Can, let's go!" Without thinking, Tang Can jumped up from the table and ran off, barely washing her hands.

Zhou Ran yelled, "Tang Can!" She turned to see that Xuan hadn't touched his breakfast. Zhou Ran kept asking about Xuan's long face from yesterday, but Xuan didn't say a word. He roughly wiped his hands on the plate and stormed off to his room, slamming the door shut behind her. Zhou Ran was left sitting in shock, the sound of the door closing still ringing in her ears. At night, Zhou Ran quietly served dinner to Tang Can and Xuan. Tang thought her mom was silent because she had run off to play without finishing her food. After finishing her supper, Tang went to her room. Xuan, on the other hand, understood why Zhou was silent. Before going to bed, he took a shower and entered his room, where he found Zhou Ran already lying in bed. Xuan approached her, to talk, but she remained quiet. Xuan then told Zhou Ran everything. She asked, "What about Tang's education?" Xuan replied, "They've arranged a new school for Can Can in Nankai." Even though everything was settled, Zhou Ran said, "Tang will be upset about this. She'll probably cry. We should keep this from her for now." Xuan agreed with her and they went to sleep. The day before New Year, Steven and Tang played at the park for a long time. Tired, they rested on a bench. Steven suggested having snacks, so instead of going home, Tang took him to DD Grandpa's flat, number thirteen. They knocked on the door and waited until DD Grandpa let them in. They asked for some snacks, but DD Grandpa made them wait a bit. He first gave them soy milk, but since Steven was allergic, he offered him herb water instead. DD Grandpa then made sweet corn cheese dumplings, Tang and Steven's favorite. They enjoyed the dumplings and drank slowly. After washing their hands, they hugged Grandpa and said, "You are the best dumpling maker in the world!" with sweet voices.

In the evening, Tang saw her mom, Zhou Ran, packing things, then Tang asked why. Zhou Ran replied that they were going to Nankai for a trip. Tang excitedly shouted with joy but then realized she would miss Steven for two days. She asked her mom if Steven could come along, but Zhou Ran sadly said no. Tang, disappointed, went to her room without having her dinner. Steven waited a long time to watch the fireworks with Tang, but since they couldn't stay up until midnight, he went to bed at ten.

On New Year's Day, Steven woke up before Tang. He quickly got ready in his new outfit and went to greet Tang. As usual, Tang slept in, but when she got up, she quickly dressed to match Steven and opened her room door. Steven had already come inside and greeted Tang's mom and dad. When Tang saw their matching outfits, she was thrilled. She jumped, ran up to Steven, and grabbed his hand, then they jumped for joy together. Steven and Tang got red pockets from Xuan. In joy, they went to Steven's house, where Steven's mom gave Tang a big chocolate and red pockets to them. After hiding the red pockets in their room. They ran up the stairs, and they discussed excitedly about buying toys with their red pockets.

They went to DD Grandpa's house, but he wasn't home. So, they raced down the stairs toward the park. On the way, some boys passed by and felt jealous of their matching pastel green dresses with twin badges of pink and blue. Steven grabbed her hand, and they ran toward the park. Once inside the children's park, she noticed DD Grandpa sitting on a wooden bench. They both went up to Grandpa and said, "Why are you sitting here, Grandpa? We looked for you at home, but you were here." Grandpa smiled and replied, "I was waiting for you both here." They asked, "Why were you waiting for us, Grandpa?" Grandpa then pulled out a Ginkgo sapling from behind the bench and handed it to them, saying it was for them to plant. They both looked at each other with excitement when they saw the sapling, thrilled to receive it as a New Year gift from Grandpa.

While Grandpa went to get a tool to dig in the sand, Tang and Steven went home to change their clothes. At Steven's house, his mom asked why he wanted to change. He told her that DD Grandpa gave them a sapling to plant. Understanding, his mom dressed him in something more suitable for gardening. Tang came out of her house and waited for Steven. Once he came out, they both headed to the park where Grandpa was waiting for them. Steven began digging in the sand while Tang helped. Afterward, Grandpa handed them the sapling, and they carefully placed it in the hole, making sure to fill the space with sand. Tang held the sapling steady while Steven filled the gap. Grandpa praised them, and they smiled proudly. To celebrate, they ran back to their homes, washed their hands grabbed their badges, and swapped them as a sign of their friendship. Steven got the pink badge from Tang, and Tang got the blue badge from him.

On New Year's Eve, Tang took out a black bracelet from her drawer. Her mom asked, "Who are you going to give that to?" Tang replied that she was going to give it to Steven as a New Year's gift. She ran to Steven's house and asked his mom where he was. His mom said he was sleeping. Tang quietly went to his room and slipped the bracelet onto his wrist. As she did, Steven woke up and looked at the bracelet with shining eyes. Steven's mom then called them for snacks. After they ate, they planned to watch the fireworks in the park with their new friend. They ran to the park and sat on a bench, waiting for the fireworks to start. While waiting, they started to get bored. Steven had an idea to give a name to their new friend, the Ginkgo plant. Tang suggested mixing their names, but Steven said, "It's our friend, so we should give him a proper name." Tang then started thinking hard about names. Suddenly, Steven opened his mouth and raised his right-hand man finger with an excited sound Ahh! Tang asked, "What is it, Steve?" Just as Steven was about to say the name, a loud noise came from the sky, followed by a burst of colors. Tang jumped up from the bench, clapping with excitement, while Steven got down and shouted, "Happy New Year!" They both looked up, their eyes wide with wonder as they watched the fireworks light up the sky.

The next afternoon, Tang Xuan and her family packed their bags and went downstairs. Tang ran to Steven's house and said, "I'm going to spend two days in Nankai." She was excited but also worried about missing Steven. Steven's family knew that Tang's father was transferring to Nankai and that they would be moving there, but Tang's parents and Steven's parents had kept it a secret from their kids. Tang took her small backpack and went outside. Steven and his parents stood outside to say goodbye. Before Tang got into the car, she told Steven, "I'll be back in two days. Don't forget to water our friend." Steven promised he would take care of the plant. As the car started to move, Tang rolled down her window and waved goodbye. Steven's eyes filled with sadness as he watched the car leave. He ran to the park, sat by the plant, and talked about Tang leaving, crying as he spoke.

Sang Yan said, *"That was the last day of their happy times."* Gal, with tears in her eyes, asked what happened next. *"Steven's family had an accident two years later. When Tang returned to see Steven, he was no longer there. Since then, she has come back every year to visit this place. Tang stayed at her aunt's house to rest."* Afterward, she gave her favorite perfume to Aunt Vivian as a New Year's gift. Vivian's face lit up with happiness and she thanked Tang for it. Just then, Tang's phone rang. While she answered the call, she walked around and eventually stepped onto the balcony. When the call ended, Vivian came out to the balcony with tea. Tang took the tea from her aunt and asked, "Aunt Vivian, when did Cypress arrive here?" As Vivian began to answer Tang, her uncle called from the kitchen to ask about the dumpling parcel, so she had to leave.

On New Year's Eve, Tang came out of her room while Vivian was cleaning the dining table. Hearing the door open, Vivian turned and was amazed by how beautiful Tang looked in her pastel green gown and matte brown lipstick. Tang's eyelashes and blush made her face glow. Vivian noticed Tang holding something, but she couldn't tell what it was. As Tang walked past, the warm scent of her Brown Homie perfume lingered in the air even after she left. She stepped out of her aunt's flat, number thirty, and went down the stairs. She walked across the pathway and into the park. There, Gal asked Sang, "How do you know all this?" Tang approached the same bench where Sang was standing. Sang replied, "I'm their friend. They sprouted me during their last happy New Year." As the fireworks burst in the sky, Tang's eyes sparkled with tears as she watched the fireworks, she opened her hand and gazed at the blue badge, and her ears were filled with the sound of Steven's voice calling out, "Sang Yan! Happy New Year!"

CHAPTER FOUR

The Grayscale Chaos

-By Amala Rachel Eliud

1.ONCE WHITE, NOW YELLOW

'Once white, now yellow', read the headlines. Grandpa sat leaning on his easy chair, with his arms stretched wide, holding the newspaper onto it. Now and then, he would emphasize on anything that overwhelmed him. He often announced promptly, "Oh what a wretched world!", because the technological innovations and the modern demeanours inundated him. And that day, it was the Taj Mahal which earned his emphasis.

"Taj Mahal, a timeless emblem of true love turns yellow. The walls look pale due to the pollution in the city", he turned silent. I walked towards him from the other side of the room and jokingly remarked, "wretched world nah thatha!". Grandpa's eyes slightly shrank and his cheeks widened, making the wrinkles wrinkle more, as a reply.

Grandpa had many stories. He was fond of telling stories about grandma. His stories were supposedly 'history'. It was by one such historical account, I came to know that paatima- that's how we called our grandma, had a childhood experience in Burma. She was born and brought up in a city named Rangoon, as the eldest in her family during the 1930s. But one day, a disaster happened and their happy family was shattered. A huge blast was heard, followed by consequent gunshots and fire explosions. People ran here and there, crying for help. Instantaneously, the colonies were wrecked up and were converted into military camps. Huge tanks and other beast-like machines took in the dwelling. Fear of death shook everybody. It was an episode of terror and bloodshed and the rest is history.

Soon, the radio gave in its hasty news. "The Japanese army invades the country. More than a hundred casualties are reported. The government insists that all the citizens should leave the country as soon as possible, as threats flood in." The reason was World War II.

Stella, my paatima's mother, was then just a thirty-three years old lady. Her husband, my paatima's father, was on duty as a telephone operator. Left alone to deal with the cruel setting, she stood helpless, however she knew that she had to do something to safeguard her four little children, all by herself. She couldn't seek help from anyone because the neighbourhood was as chaotic as her little mind. My paatima was a twelve-year-old girl at that time, who had an active ease that came as a compliment to her youthful sense. She couldn't help but stood in utter amazement as she witnessed the town's sudden metamorphosis. Although she was too young to understand all about wars and migrations, she could sense the anxiety of her dear mother, whose affectionate eyes which always had a kind and soft look now gave a varied stillness, giving direct insights to her confused soul. As the eldest child, paatima had the protective instincts that came to her naturally and she ran towards her mother to help her with anything she could.

With the aid of her eldest daughter, Stella could take only a little provision and managed to sweep her children out of the house. Thankfully, she heard a message from her husband through his best friend Agathus, who hurried her to the railroad station. So, she joined with the other ladies, disappearing into the rush.

As many as the stories, grandpa also treasured some handwritten letters, stacked in a small cardboard box. Those were like his licensed proofs, which he showed us at times during his story narrations. Most of the collection included his letters to paatima and her letters to him. Grandma's handwriting was explicitly elegant and in turn he projected his calligraphy excellence in the front pages. The papers have turned so brittle and were too fragile. 'Once white, now yellow'.

Few other letters were from someone named Victoz. Thatha said that he was a 'younger brother who always felt like home'. His letters were also one of the most valued stuffs owned by thatha.

Oh, the rush, the emotions that even just a letter held, made my heart thump so hard. "But would it be anywhere near to what Stella paama would have felt on that day?", I pondered. (I don't honestly remember why I call my paatima's mother as 'paama', But we fondly followed this as one of our family traditions for generations.) Amidst the riotous setting, she somehow made it to the train. The ladies had to please her to do that act of bravery for the sake of her kids. Yet her eyes longed to find her husband among the rushing crowd. She gazed through the window, holding onto her youngest child, who was just a few months old. Suddenly, a voice from the crowd called "Stella!". Her amusement grew as she stood up and looked out to see her husband calling. Dramatic enough, the train started its baffled journey. And before she could make a decision, his trembling voice cried, "Listen Stella... I'll see you soon in India ... just be strong- and don't be worried! Stella, I'll see you soon!", the volume of his cries slowly diminished, leaving Stella in absolute tears. She wheezed as she cried out loud holding her four children close to her and embracing them tightly. On that very moment, she felt like she was holding her entire world and was not ready to lose any parts, anymore. The train pressed down to India and nobody had a happy journey that day.

But Stella knew that she had to brace herself up. She knew that it was going to be hard to return to the country which she had left almost fourteen years ago. They had some relatives in India, but it had been such a long time that even navigating them would definitely be a Herculean task for her. However, she had no other choice than doing it all single-handedly because her husband was a government employee who had other responsibilities back in the land. Thankfully, she had a little dollar chain dancing down from her neck. With that she could provide her little ones. Days must have been hard for them who had nothing else, other than their very body and soul to carry through.

Little did paama know on that day that she would never be back to Burma again and she would find faith, God and life in India. Through it all, the question kept pestering her. "Will he make it to the next train or at least the last train to India?". The journey continued to the still darkness.

"Aren't you gonna be late for college Ethan?", grandpa softly roared as I quickened up to the present and headed out shouting "bye thatha!". He smiled as he waved me goodbye. The share-auto dropped me off near the metro station which was two kilometres away from home. I was inwardly bracing myself for the new day's adventure, as I paid my fare with a hesitant eye contact. As I was walking through the subway, I saw many different people with many distinct stories, while some were told; some were hidden; some were shared and some were still secrets. They were all walking just like me. And I passed them all with neither an idea nor a reaction, just as a passing cloud.

As soon as I hopped in the metro, I took my book out to read, because I had to pass a solid and lonely forty minutes locked up in this giant cart. Moreover, it was always a pleasure for me to read Dickens. I was so in passionate adoration to his beautiful narration.

'I saw that everything within my view which ought to be white, had been white long ago, and had lost its lustre, and was faded and yellow', the author's lines hit deeper into my soul. It reminded me of thatha's accordion. Both despite being old, never lost its essence. Did I just forget to mention that grandpa could play the accordion? It was literally one classic move that he made to outshine the others in town. Rather he often played it to impress my paatima after she was engaged to him.

Once when my mom was cleaning up the attic-like storage space in our home, we found Thatha's dear accordion wrapped up in old newspapers and clothes. It majestically sat inside a gigantic trunk box. His face lit up as he saw it. I noticed that the keys turned a bit yellowish due to the time's test. 'Once white, now yellow': they were perfectly arranged.

I was too curious to ask thatha to play it for me. "Oh! but the keys would be out of tune dear!", he remarked. But only later I realised that it was not about the keys. He stopped playing it since she was gone. It was about her; about grandma.

It was music that connected them. I remember once thatha saying that paatima was a harpist. How soulful their connection would have been! But was it more than how Stella paama felt- all glued up to her little munchkins? To dear life she felt like she was meant to protect them.

"When did the train reach India, thatha?", I asked.

"Never" grumped thatha.

"What? but grandma was in there; what about paama and her kids?"

The sizzling fact that paama's world never found shape startled me. But thatha maintained his peace and said, "The rail track was blocked halfway through the journey.

The train never made it to India. But God's hand was still with your grandma." Quite relieved by the statement, I made myself comfy in the couch. Contradictorily, thatha's tone had changed a bit seriously, "And for the rest of the journey, they walked."

As hard as it sounded, paama and her petite family had a struggled march. But considering the cold December nights and that she barely had any necessities to support her pilgrimage towards hope, I could obviously witness her will-power.

And they walked those three-hundred miles or so, just as an allusion of Exodus. Paama took the few clothes she packed and made her kids wear them one over the other, like a pile of multi-layered clothing. So that if one of the clothes got dirty, they would just remove and throw that away. This was a quick discovery made by the migrating ladies to avoid carrying so much luggage. Eventually everybody adapted to the technique.

On their way, there were now and then some underground tunnel caves, designed for providing the migraters some bare necessities - especially food, like bread and fruits and also water. When there was any sign that the military forces were likely to fire a bomb, there would be a huge siren call. The travellers were alerted by the caution and they would just get into the nearest tunnel for their safety at such instances.

This terrific routine was continued until paama and the other fleers safely marched towards India. And almost after eight months of constant trying, her husband managed to return back to his family and his native land.

Yes! He made it to India. It made me happy that their story had a happy ending.

Paatima's parents had a happy story. "But thatha, how do you and paatima met?", my question made his wrinkles more wrinkled as he said, "Oh! That's another big story" and he laughed it off.

Whilst my racing thoughts, the metro's door opened and I got off. I strived to pace up because I was running late. My college was just opposite the station which made it so much easier to me in such cases, always.

As soon as I entered the huge campus, ordained with the bright green trees, a fresh yet heavy breeze whooshed over me. Suddenly, a sharp sound of my name startled me from afar. I looked up to see Talent, and my friend came running to me. He was breathing heavily, trying to tell me something. Before I could enquire much, I saw that his eyes were red and tear-filled. He almost seemed to bawl his eyes out.

His such conduct frightened me even more as I shook him asking, "What happened Tal?... Is everything alright...?"

"No", he cried like his whole world was collapsing. I couldn't tolerate anymore and kept asking him the same thing, until he finally gave in,

"Sundhar uncle didn't make it." A vague statement that made everything stop. That one sentence made every little thing around me somehow turn immobile and motionless. I could see Tal trying to relieve me. He kept calling my name and patting my face. But I was too numb to process, too much in shock to respond.

Sundhar uncle was our dearest watchman uncle, whom we loved the most. His gentle smile and his humble gaze were too sweet to put in words. Nobody ever welcomed us like that. He had the aura to create a thousand good things. With just that innocent smile, he did wonders. Everybody loved him.

But the cruel cancer chased him. And one day he stopped coming to college and was hospitalized. We raised funds to support him, we arranged prayer chains and made frequent hospital visits to cheer him up. We wanted to give him back the smiles which he gave us. But he didn't make it.

Tal tried to convince me, "Everything is meant to pass away Eth... Either good or bad... The end has no bars!". I let him finish the sentence. His lines hit directly into my soul.

But when I returned home that day, nothing was the same as it was before. "So, this is it? Everything will reach its last day someday. Nothing remains and nothing stays?" I rushed towards thatha's room. The blue walls with the photographs hanging on them were telling infinite stories from the nineteen forties. The accordion found its place in the top shelf, loftily seated to witness the whole setting. The flower vases and the Bible verses radiated the place. Thatha sat amidst it all in his easy chair having his daily talk with God.

I had a burning thought that conquered my mind like consuming flames.

Someday, the walls and the signs would fade,

the letters and the memories would grow old,

the wedding gown and flowers would wither,

the keys of the accordion would turn pale.

All that was once white would turn yellow.

But, love never did search for any colours to change...

So, should I tell you how my thatha and my paatima actually met each other?

2. BEAUTIFUL IN BLUE

It was just another humdrum Tuesday when the realization hit me like a storm. And ever since then, my subconscious mind bears that horrible thought that could never be undone anymore. I went to thatha's room to give him his evening tea. We shared a simple smile and then he said, "thank you dear!" When I looked into his face, I was grasped by his eyes. I realized that his pupils were kind of shrinking recently. A shiny yet dull ash circle filled the outer layer of his eyeball. His gaze has changed. It was a probable change in the old age, but was so hard for us to get used to.

It came to me like a flash, that thatha was getting old. Sank by the horrid fact, I looked at him once again, who was slowly sipping out from the tea cup. His round glasses were seated on the top of the nose. His hair turned all white yet neatly cropped and combed. His clear shaved face highlighted his wrinkles.

Thatha turned ninety-five this year, an age which was unbelievable to many- particularly me. Though aged, he was blessed enough to be independent in doing his regular routines and could walk on his own, within the home. Only outside, he needed a little support. Everybody said that it is far too great for his age. But I was still struck by the change and couldn't process that his walks became slower, his voice grew softer and his grip, when he held my hands became too feeble. All of a sudden, everything was changed.

"Ethan", the former mentioned feeble voice crackled, "take that photo frame", his gentle hands were pointing to one of the many other portraits in the room. By that time, he was done with his tea and had switched his interest towards the tidiness of his treasures. "It's a bit dusty, get me a cloth dear, let me clean it", he continued.

"I'll do that thatha", I fetched it from him and wiped the frame with a little piece of cloth.

As I was wiping the photo frame, thatha remarked, "Do you know when it was taken? It was our wedding day. See how gloriously we were posing!" I gave him an excited expression however I was well aware of it already. As thatha was affected by partial memory loss recently, that came with his age, he tended to repeat some things again and again for a concerning amount of time. I never wanted to impede his curiosity, so every single time, I pretended like I heard it for the first time.

Through the little frame, the young couple smiled at me. The lad showed a happier face, with a triumphant gaze. One of his eyebrows was slightly lifted and the other one tried to stay calm. The former extroverted brow contrasted the latter bashful one. The silent battle between those two was obvious in his expressive countenance. His hair, though it was a monochrome picture, was seemingly black, combed neatly straight upwards, creating a sort of elevated platform upon his head.

Beside him was the young lady, with the sweetest and calming smile. Her face, slightly tilted, picturing a view of her perfect big bun. Her little curls escaped from her perfected hairdo and fell down to her forehead, not outshining her face but complimented it in the softest way possible. Her eyes were full of life, which too smiled, directly into mine. She was wearing a superficially bright white saree, supposedly. Perhaps, it was not a demandable fact, since it was a black and white picture.

The glass frame glimmered a bit, highlighting the wedding year which was mentioned in the corner: '1953'. I glanced at the couple and then the year for a while, holding the photograph carefully. And then I pulled my chair to get closer to thatha and asked keenly, "how was life back then, thatha?"

He stared at me vaguely and asked, "back when?"

"Post-war and pre-wedding! Was it the best of times or the worst of times?", I sharply intended, expecting another story from him.

"A beautiful mess... filled with the works of love, God's will and time!", as he proposed the philosophical statement, he gently stood up and clutched the frame from my hands and proceeded to hang it onto its ordained place, amidst all the other chosen masterpieces.

I was rather disappointed by the unexpected 'long story short' version from him.

"Tell me your story, thatha... or just any other story", I pleaded.

Thatha gave a little smirk while he sat down on his easy chair, letting out a deep audible sigh. As I was intrigued seeing the positive sign from him, thatha went on with the narration of the story and I melted into my own fantasy of picturing his words.

In my little mind, the scene shifted to sometime near 1940. "One... two- three, four:"..., a whispering voice persisted in counting the pigeons with his little feet tiptoed, looking up from the balcony.

"Levi, the breakfast is ready... come on down", a loud voice interrupted.

"Coming Maa!", the eleven-year-old little boy responded, almost in an equally high volume while he ran downstairs to the kitchen. His mother was making 'surul-appam', a common south-Indian breakfast.

Down in the dark kitchen, he watched his mother pour a ladle full of wheat batter onto the pan and spread it all over its circumference. The corners turned a bit brown after a while of waiting, then she carefully placed two spoons of the coconut and sugar mixture over it and rolled the appam perfectly. Once it was done, she packed them into a small box and continued, "Here Levi! Be careful on your way to school."

The town was located in the outskirts of Pune, which was not so much affected by the growing civilization, but was partly developing. Levi had to walk to school, which was located in the city, some miles away. When he got out of the semi-detached house which was painted in dull tones, he was anxious and scared.

As Levi's father was a military officer, 'transfers' were not new to the family. Additionally, since it was the world war times, they always awaited a post modification or a transfer at every nook and corner, although the situation was thoroughly unwelcomed. By one such unwelcomed shift, the family moved to Pune. It was almost two years ago, but still 'going to school' haunted Levi.

After walking for almost half the way, he momentarily stopped. The embodiment of his fear was before him. A group of five to six kids stood before him like a semi-circular fence, all looking at him fiercely. They had some sticks and stones. Levi took a step back. One of the kids said, "hey, see who's here... the music boy huh". His comment was followed by the crowd's laugh. It was just another bully encounter for Levi, who was too scared to respond. Every day at school, he was called the 'music boy', because they considered that he was soft and timid to play music. They mocked him and called him with names. Sometimes, they even beat him up for fun. They would even go to the extent of pouring water on him and locking him up in empty classrooms.

Levi was trembling, his body gave him chills. He was sweating profusely, knowing that he was their object of ridicule now. And as his trembling hands raised in reflex to defend himself in the most possible way, he heard a loud continuous noise from behind. "Ammaaa is coming...You caught! You all caught...", he realised that the voice was Lily's. She ran towards the small pack as she was holding her big bag like a shield. But she tripped and fell down before she could get near them. The kids were afraid that some elders would come and decided to flee away. By that time, both Levi and Lily were at the ground.

Levi quickly got his feet to the ground and ran to help Lily. Lily was Levi's little sister, who was just two years younger than him. He had other three little brothers, who were too small to go to school. "Why did you run so fast? It is so dangerous.", he asked, although he definitely knew the answer for the 'why', but as the eldest of the family, he was meant to be protective. "Are you hurt?", he added with a solid, grim face. "No!", she faintly replied. Levi turned silent. He suddenly clutched her hands and led the way towards school. For Lily, just like me, Levi was still a hero: no matter what.

"So, you were bullied in your school. New information thatha!", my comment impeded his flow. "How do you know that it's my story -", he sounded a bit disappointed. "Oh! thatha it is obvious." He looked keenly unto me as I said that. After a few silent seconds, he laughed, "Oh God, you are a clever boy, Eth!" My heart couldn't hold on from the beautiful thought of how innocent this old man was! I asked in wonder, "Only except that you were called Levi– Is your name not Robert?". "Levi Roberts- that's my complete name!", he instantly put it on.

Thatha said that one particular day in Pune, he came back from school to a sweet surprise. His little siblings were so excited to tell him about that. His mother was busy packing things and arranging them. Father was not home but was expected to return soon. Yes, they were moving again, just one another transfer. But this time, they were permanently shifting to their native place in Tamilnadu. His brothers had never been there before and were expecting a lot. Lily was busy collecting all her toys, making sure not to leave anything behind. Levi only had a blurred memory of the place. But inwardly he was so happy, his soul felt relieved to finally see an escapade from his bullies.

With the excitement in the air, the family packed their whole life in suitcases and jute sacks. Their journey towards Kadhaiyoor was explicit with hope and laughter filled in their hearts. After three long days of travel, the train has reached the destination. The bullock cart dropped them off in the long-awaited hometown. The whole setting was so relaxing and stunning. The place was filled with many trees. Little houses were lined up on each side of the tiny streets. It was comparatively a small village, but Levi felt like it was more welcoming.

The narrow streets stretched long to the end. The village consisted of only three streets, some had many houses, and some had only a few. The end of each street was connected altogether to an empty ground, in which a big banyan tree stood upright, while plenty of its children surrounded it circularly. The village church was at the right corner of the ground. It was a small building and had a tile roof. A big cross was placed at the top of the building, which was connected to the church bell. The village was paralleled by two other similar sized villages. The church was the common place for the flaunting trio. Although small, the village had a gigantic gate, which Levi thought was a symbol of protection and at the same time, diversity. Sadly, that's how the world revolves.

Thatha's eyes gleamed as he said, "The sky was so blue on that day. So wide, so calm and so blue. It was beautiful". Only then I had a striking realisation of how thatha was so in admiration for the colour blue. He said that it was a heavenly colour. And just so you know, paatima's wedding dress was not white as I thought. It was blue. Because it has been at least fifteen instances since thatha had repeated this same phrase,

"Our wedding day was glorious and she was beautiful in blue..."

It was because of this dementia that had made him to repeat the things which were engraved in the deepest parts of his heart, over and over again. Those repetitions included his timeless pure love for paatima.

He smiled again, "she was beautiful in the heavenly blue".

3. TRAIL OF THE CRIMSON BUTTERFLIES

The petit village was everything that Levi and his little siblings dreamed about. It met all of his eleven-year-old fantasies and expectations. Everything was great- except one thing. The same thing that haunted him pursued to haunt him further. Only the reason for the deed was different, but the deed stayed. Levi was bullied by the kids in the village. But music was not their concern, his stammers were their mock toy.

Levi's mother was explicitly religious. She used to drag her kids to church every Sunday. When the church bell made its call at six in the evening, she expected her kids to kneel down and pray, right away. Although her mechanical actions were not truly projecting her belief in the truth, she was pretty traditional in doing those as a regular routine. Her such conduct earned Levi a place in the church orchestra.

The situation was just an add-on of fuel to the burning flames. Because after the practice sessions, he was teased and was bullied even more. Despite the hardships, Levi managed to make some friends in the village. But that didn't change any of his bully encounters. When all of the kids played in the big ground, chatting and running, Levi preferred to stay silent under the huge banyan tree, practicing his accordion. Only if the bullies were spotted in the scene, he would hide himself to stay safe.

Three years passed, but life was still the same. But then one day, during the usual practice session, an intrusion happened. Relieved by the unexpected break, the choir broke into a sudden burst of chats. Levi veered away from the accordion to observe the chaos. He noticed that the lady who interrupted, had a tired face but was cheerfully speaking something to the conductor inaudibly. Behind her was a little girl, partially trying to hide herself with the maroon saree of her mother, but occasionally gave a gaze to the small band and a smile to the conductor.

And then the mother proceeded to walk out the church, the conductor directed the little girl to the gigantic harp. She somehow managed to climb up the stool to reach the instrument. She was too small in front of it. But when the conductor gave the sign for her entry, her hands gracefully danced through those strings, bringing out a surprising euphony. The choir joined in and the other instruments accompanied with the flow, while Levi played too, being deeply intensified by the soulful music. At times, the harp and the accordion duo exchanged awkward eye contacts, when the wrong note was played. However, they continued to mend the same with some music magic.

Sooner, it became the talk of town that the family of the harp girl fled from Burma to here, their own land. The village had a new entry to its clan. That was not just the new thing in town. It was as rare as if the alto got the melody in a four-part choir, that Levi found a new friend for himself, in a short period of time. However, this time the acquaintance was achieved because of his bullies.

Just a week after the Burma family's arrival in the village, the expected bullying happened to Levi, during his usual quiet hours under the banyan tree. But quite weirdly, he was saved by the harp girl. The noble act was that she made her caterpillar crawl over one of the plumpy kids in the group. He was super disgusted and scared, his countenance changed as he tried to tap it off with his hands.

To his utter failure, the determinant caterpillar found its comfort in his ears and decided to stay there. The escalation of the situation brought tears to the little boy. He cried as he tried to knock it off again and again. But it transferred its place to another kid's head. The other kids bounced up and down in fear, some ran away. Everybody started crying eventually.

Contradictorily, Levi and the harp girl stood unaffected, away from the commotion. The little girl even cracked a smile as if she was finding a sort of evil peace in the chaos. After a moment of the tearful struggle, the caterpillar landed safely on the ground. The girl went forward as if it's her time to perform and held it with ease and she secured it in her tiny pocket.

The scared band ran away, crying and wheezing all along. It was just Levi and the girl, left in the place. Almost equally feared by the acts of the latter, he stammered, "Thanks!... for helping me out __"

She smiled, "Dorcas".

Levi gave an awkward, confused look as he continued, "that's my name- what's yours?".

He said, "Oh- Levi, no Roberts- Levi Roberts!"

"You let those brats put you down?... Chin up a bit more lad! Perhaps you can get some caterpillars from me- if you want", she went on without a pause.

"No, no- no, no, no ... I'm scared to even hold it", he chuckled.

"Easy; practice makes any Levi perfect", and that made both of them laugh.

The grimness of the conversation slowly slipped into the light discussion of her butterfly taming hobby. It turned out that those disgusting caterpillars were the ones which would grow into beautiful crimson butterflies. She brought them with a great effort and care, all the way from Burma in a small glass jar. And then she shared about how her siblings would be disgusted to touch her bed or even her plate because of her intensified craze for insects.

Eventually, their bond grew thicker and stronger over years. Thus, everybody's Burma girl and somebody's harp girl became the butterfly girl for Levi alone.

The days when I used to sit for hours beside thatha, who gave me insights to the chaos of the grayscale were undeniably beautiful. His stories always had a spark, a life that deserved great preservation. The soul of thatha's stories would live in my mind forever. Cause, he has left them in a good place where no demon and no dementia could destroy the life, that those stories hold.

'And, I would do anything, I would go any far, I would spare any part of me to turn over things and go back to that humdrum Tuesday- just another humdrum Tuesday'.

The reflection of the past perplexed my present. I felt that my life had turned into an uncanny episode, lately. Nothing was the same as it was before. I grew numb and it was becoming evident over time. One such numb day, when my mind had multiple emotions processing in itself, another strange thing happened. It would be an over-explainable story necessarily under-explained to say that I was almost hit by a car. Although it was partially my mistake, Talent was infuriated and was ready to fight. But the driver was an old man, he looked at least ninety years old, which made us both meltdown in peace.

The man got down from his car and expressed that he was extremely sorry. To alleviate the situation, I said that it was no big issue and assured that I was completely fine. But he was not easy to leave us and even insisted on taking us to the cafe for a nice pastry treat. Initially, I refused, partly because I didn't want to put him through such difficulty, but wholly because of a selfish reason of not wanting to die. How pathetic it would be to escape a car crash but end up being dead due to poisoning- that too, on the same day! It was the work of my overthinking. However, Tal was completely lured by the very word 'pastry' and literally nagged me to accept the offer.

That was how we ended up in the nearest cafe with a stranger, whom we just met a few hours before. The man was too advanced for his age. He was enthusiastic and his face had a cheerful aura. He wore suspenders which held his pants up to his shoulders. He wore bright coloured socks and sports shoes and an old-fashioned watch, which seemed a bit off of his style. His Maruti 800 looked well maintained and based on the past experiences, it was obvious to me that he was used to rash driving. He handled his Nokia mobile like a pro. Above everything, he asked us to call him 'gramps', the name which he recently found online.

Within a few moments, we were captivated by his innocence. He reminded me of Sundhar uncle in one way and my thatha in many ways. I felt like something about the chats with gramps could heal my soul. The strange encounter made us want to meet more times. Ever since then, the three of us had coffee, chats and some silly fun, almost every weekend with our crazy routine of meetings.

In another timeline, Levi and Dorcas had a pure friendship that blossomed along the tales of Kadhaiyoor. But uncertainty was sadly an inevitable entity that flipped over everything. Levi's father was a drunkard. Everybody knew that he was not himself when he's drunk. One morning, Levi and his family woke up to the news that startled their lives ever after. His father had sold everything that belonged to them, the house, the lands, the mill which they owned and every other single property. He wrote a will to some man, who was from the paralleling village. The family inherited almost all of the village, but due to the horrible and unconscious decision of the family's head, it was all gone in the matter of a single night. To make things worse, Levi's father fled away from the place, leaving a less detailed letter, deciding to abandon his home, wife and children for his 'find of pleasure'.

With no time to even process, Levi was forced into the position of taking responsibilities. The graveness of the situation was heavy for an eighteen-year-old. But, being the eldest of the family and the need to provide for his mother and four little siblings, he naturally stepped out and started looking for a job. The quest was not easy for Levi, he was rejected multiple times due to many reasons and one among them was his 'stammers'.

Compelled by the sudden burden of breadwinning, he moved to Chennai for the want of a job. Leaving his family at a young age was not easy for anyone, but the chaos could be only put to at least a slight difference, only if he could earn something. He didn't care to inform Dorcas about his decision, at first. But he had a striking hope that she would understand and would be there for his family during such tough times. She indeed waited for him near the banyan tree in vain. But as he knew, she went to his home once she heard about his moving. Lily ran over to her and embraced her at the door. Dorcas let Lily to cry her heart out, hoping that it would help. The family was broken into thousands of pieces. But everything that Dorcas could do was holding their hands tightly and repeating, "God knows", with tears.

A new place with the buzz of growing modernization made Levi feel as a tiny creature. Yet he was determined to walk every cubbyhole. Despite failures and rejections, he was initially full of perseverance to push himself further. But apparently everything has an end. When the day began to end, the little money in his pocket drained away, he was desperate with no place to go, no shelter to seek and no food to eat. He stared into the blank space, sitting on a park bench. Amidst the chaos, he spotted a crimson butterfly, which was returning home. "Even the trail of the butterflies is known by the Creator", his mother's words were clearly ringing in his ears. He knew very well that the next step was not in his hands and silently cried in pain.

4. SILVER LININGS

Amidst the gloomy confusions, "Hello brother", a youthful voice called from behind. Quite used to being interrupted in everything, Levi turned around with red, teary eyes. The lad gently enquired about his whereabouts and asked what was the issue. Levi was already taken aback by the chaotic turns in life and poured out everything to him. After the absurd confession to the stranger, he was bracing himself for being judged. But surprisingly, the man maintained a peaceful smile and asked Levi to stay in his home.

Trusting a stranger was the last of all the feasible things that Levi had thought of. But every other thing in the list was cut down, leaving him to follow the lad, to his place. On their way, the man cheerfully talked about so many things, he introduced himself as Victoz. He said that he had no family and his parents were killed in the migration. From a very young age, he lived there alone, earning a meagre money, just to fill his stomach. Levi wondered about the disparity between the man's life and his attitude. He also said that he was passionate about writing and hoping that he could make a life out of his poetry, someday.

By the time his story was told, they reached their destination to the tiny dwelling. The room was too little to hold the two of them. But what really mattered was Victoz's pure thought of giving and Levi's grateful heart, even though they both were struggling at their own pace. It was a seventy square feet single room, which had some belongings of the outwardly happy man. But little did Levi know that his dreams would find its shape there. Thatha said that one of the initial life givers to his dreams was the hope insisted through the words of Victoz, "Don't worry about the rent, until things become a bit stable. It's on me". It was indeed superficial for me to believe.

With the newfound hope, Levi started looking for a job more intensely. He took any petite work offered to him, from even buying chai for the workers in big companies, to loading and cleaning. He sent every penny to his family, except for a very little for himself. Through it all, Victoz was all his strength, who selflessly supported him. Levi's heart was pounding every time when Victoz offered him something, but left with no other choice, he regretfully approved. His friend's relentless shielding and his family's desperate needs made Levi keep running.

I had a clear picture of a particular encounter with thatha in my mind. He said, "Silver linings are for the world, God's paintings are for us." It was indeed proved in every episode of his life. And not only in passion and dreams, but also in the true faith in God, the young men grew.

Based on Victoz's original idea, Levi applied for a job in the railways. Things got weird for the duo, when he unexpectedly got the job, after the messed-up interview. Both of them were ecstatic and shocked at the same time. The job brought so much difference in both of their lives. Levi wanted to repay for everything he got from Victoz, in some way. The kind soul of his friend deserved every bit of happiness. So, he decided to secretly apply his name for the Art school selection in Pune. And as days passed by, he forgot about that eventually. Years flew away, Age and friendship grew in both the timelines.

I had a scheduled meeting that day, at six in the evening with Talent and Gramps. The cafe was our usual spot. Tal and myself, initially accepted these meetings to give Gramps some company. He occasionally insisted, "you look exactly like my grandson", which over time felt like a compliment to us. But after a few days, we started finding tranquillity in such gatherings. Gramps was an amazing poet. He enthusiastically brought all his unpublished and even unread poems to us. When we didn't understand some imagery and connotations, he gladly explained that. His eyes gleamed with passion, every single time.

"The colour of war

The colour of love's design-

Was it grayscale,

Transcending the timeline?" ...

"Sir, there's someone in the office to meet you", the peon announced. Levi left the papers aside and went out unhurriedly. Through the glass window, he could see two grave figures lingering outside the office door. When he reached them, he was more than just surprised. The old man smiled from ear to ear as he saw him. Levi energetically said, "Uncle! How are you?". He walked steadily unto him and held his hands. The man replied, "we all are fine thambi, it has been so long since we met..." The duo proceeded to embrace each other, whilst exchanging greetings. After a short while of the encounter, Levi looked at the other person, who stood still with no proper expressions. "How are you, Dorcas? You haven't changed a bit still... Every crimson butterfly I saw here, reminded me of you...", Levi wanted to blab his heart out to her, but for the need of showing respect to her father, he forcefully stopped himself with a smile. His friendship with her stayed still fresh and unaffected in his mind.

The man continued, "Dorcas just got a job in the telephone office. I'm leaving her alone in this town only because of you. Please take care of her". Those simple words of trust melted Levi who assured him that he would definitely keep his words. The man and his daughter left after a few instances of conversation. Levi asked them to join him for lunch but they gently denied.

After two days of the meeting, Levi decided to make a visit to Dorcas' workplace, just to make sure that she was fine and comfortable. But secretly inwards, he wanted to ask her how all those years have been, as he hoped for the old friendly reunion. When she was announced of his arrival, she quietly walked towards him and gravely said, "why are you here?".

"Oh... to make sure if things are right with you! Are you feeling any hardships here?"

"You don't have to do that". His smile faded by the grim response.

"Listen, I don't want to be disrespectful. But let me make this clear for you. I've asked my father many times not to come standing at your doorstep- not to a man who never wrote nor at least cared to inform, all these years", her voice was shaking as she continued, "I know how to take care of myself. You don't have to worry 'bout it." She walked away leaving Levi shattered in regret.

That evening, Victoz noticed the sudden disappointment that was evident in Levi's countenance, when he got home. Upon questioning, Levi explained the whole situation to him. Levi realised that it was obviously his own mistake, that he didn't respect the value of their friendship. Victoz tried to help by proposing an idea to mend the issue, "Write to her! It must help".

So, Levi proceeded with the idea, after so many days of rethinking. He didn't know what to write but finally went on with, "do you still tame crimson butterflies? If not, please do. Because I could only find a very few of them now..." he was not altogether confident about the message and wrote at the back of the postcard, "if this letter makes you madder, please know that it was my friend's idea, not mine."

The post reached Dorcas' workplace. Without her knowledge, a smile cracked through her lips as she read the postscript. She wrote him back, "I do tame them still. Sooner, they'll paint the town with silver linings... Also, I think that even your friend knows, that practice can make any Levi perfect!" Victor was right though. His idea made wonders. Their bond started to reform through many letters, once again.

Those three had their time in the town. It was sometime in the 1950s. But then one day they received a letter. Not the usual ones, but a recruitment offer. All three were shocked when they realized that it was the selection list for the writing course in the Art school. Even Levi couldn't believe that his secret action had turned into a positive reply.

The incident made both Levi and Victoz fall into utter bafflement. They were extremely happy but were too stunned to respond. Levi thought the best for Victoz, he would be more than just happy if his friend followed his passion all along. That was indeed his pride. But on the other hand, he was not ready to lose him. Victoz just wanted and longed, his whole life for that one thing - his passion. And when it became real, he could not wholly be satisfied. He was too scared to leave Levi. The gravity of the situation made them both silent for a while.

After one whole day of deep silence, they both gave up themselves to confess. When they both realized the similarity of their mindsets, they cried their hearts out. The day when Victoz was leaving for Pune arrived. The episode was filled with tears, joy, hugs, and goodbyes. The train slowly moved, and Dorcas and Levi were seen waving a long and painful farewell to their dearest friend, a friend who always felt at home.

It was ridiculous to me how tangled the timeline was. It pauses, it replays, it forwards, it speeds up, just as it pleases. The tales of the grayscale were in fact pure chaos, just like my thoughts that race over nothing.

When the grayscale glimmers faded away, I found myself again in the same old present. "You are so good in poetry, gramps", Tal remarked. "I don't take credit for my writings altogether. Firstly, it is all 'alms from above' and then it is because of a God-sent friend, who felt like home", brightly said Gramps. The power of words confused me as I knew that I'd already heard those same words from somewhere else. Gramps gloriously smiled as he continued, "That fellow recruited me in art school. He gave me his brand-new watch when we parted ways. It has his name inscribed onto it." He laughed, "That guy... he stopped writing to me, of course, he must have lost my address!" I was more than just shocked. Tal seemed to enjoy his story but I sat there like a statue, frozen by what I thought. Gramps took out his hands from his pockets to look at the time from his old-fashioned watch. His face gave a frozen grin. I felt the current of my blood escalates in speed. My brain shut itself down and I fainted, as I saw the letters inscribed near the watch dial, "Levi".

Somehow, one part of Thatha's stories was still alive.

Or, Was it just another race –- of my thoughts?

CHAPTER FIVE

Susurration of a Hidden Soul

-By Aramvalarthasivagami. R

It was a breezy April day, the green leaves swaying gently in the air. A black-haired boy with misty blue-framed spectacles carefully approached the front door, trying to unlock it without a sound. In his left hand, he hid something behind his back. Quietly slipping off his shoes and into his slippers, he tiptoed through the hallway. As he passed the kitchen, he glanced in, making sure his mother was busy with her work. Satisfied she hadn't noticed him, he slipped into his room and softly locked the door behind him, all without a single noise.

With a cheerful smile, he wiped down his study table, still scattered with remnants of brown gift wrap, and carefully placed the newly unwrapped gift on its surface. His room was bathed in soft pastel green paint. Had each wall adorned with posters of "Best of DD Love Poems," carefully curated by him. The single bed, near a bookshelf, was strewn with fresh clothes. On the study table sat a white lamp, a bottle of water, a writing tool holder, and a few books. His eyes sparkled with excitement as he quickly tore open the brown gift cover and embraced the book. It was a castle-green volume titled 'Susurration of a Hidden Soul', a collection of poems by DD. He flipped eagerly through the first few pages, he closed his eye screen and chose a page, his heart racing, and his lips started to read the poem,

In the race between my heart's beat and breath,

I lost my rhythm to reach her heart.

She took the pulse that once ran wild and free,

And turned it still.

She tamed my red-blooded heart, entwined with tender strings.

And forged it gently into a heart stone ring.

Now in her hand, my soul, a quiet thing,

Adorns her finger as a sacred ring.

Without a word, she flew from where she'd been

Leaving only silence!

After reading the poem, his eyes began to fill with tears, and he was left speechless. Just then, his mother knocked on the door, calling, "Karthick, Karthick, I know you're in there. Open up." Called his mother with anger. Panicking, he quickly wiped away his tears, shoved the book into his closet, and relaxed his shoulders, trying to appear normal before opening the door.

His mother asked what he was doing. He started to stammer, unable to form a proper answer, and she immediately noticed his pale expression. Her eyes shifted to the half-closed closet. Without a word, she motioned for him to step aside and walked into the room. Beads of sweat appeared on his face as she opened the closet fully. There, she found DD's love poem book. Her eyes flashed with anger as she turned to him, and he stood frozen with panic. She took the book, left the room, and sat down on the cozy crimson sofa in the living room.

Her silence made Karthick feel like a fish out of water. He nervously stepped forward and stood in front of her, but she turned her face away, refusing to meet his gaze. Stammering, he began to apologize for not following her rules. Karthick's mother, deeply concerned about his growing interest in love poems, had warned him countless times to avoid them. Yet his fascination with DD's poems had become irresistible. Despite living in Greenwich, London, their family held onto strict, orthodox values. And to make matters more delicate, it was his eighteenth birthday.

His mother finally broke the silence, her voice firm but gentle. "Karthick, we moved here for your dad's job, but your future will be in India. This is a crucial age, one where distractions like these can pull you away from your studies. That's why I'm so worried about your obsession with love poems. I hope you understand where we're coming from. Today is your birthday, and I don't want to ruin it for you, but let this be your final warning. Don't do this again." She gave him a stern look before setting the book aside.

Karthick muttered under his breath, a hint of frustration in his voice, before reluctantly saying sorry. He wanted to argue with his mother, but at the same time, he didn't. Casting a longing glance at the book, he sighed and stepped out of the house. Once outside, he kicked a stone in frustration, still muttering angrily to himself. After pacing back and forth a couple of times, his gaze fell on the house across the street, where an old man lived—someone from his hometown in India.

Feeling a need for comfort, Karthick crossed the road and rang the doorbell. Through the peephole, a watchful eye confirmed it was him, and the door swung open. The old man greeted him with a smile. His bald head gleamed under the light, while his neatly trimmed French beard added a distinguished touch. Dressed in a blue T-shirt and black trousers, he radiated warmth.

"Hey, Karthick! Happy birthday, young man! So, where's my birthday chocolate?" the old man said with a teasing grin.

Noticing Karthick's frustration, the old man stopped his playful chatter and motioned for him to sit on the living room sofa. Karthick often sought comfort in his company whenever he felt down. Though they always sat in the old man's backyard, sharing whatever was on their minds, Karthick had never asked his name. The old man, however, never seemed to mind, allowing Karthick to roam freely around the house—except for his bedroom.

Sensing Karthick's mood, the old man headed to the kitchen to prepare a glass of fresh grape juice, knowing it was his favorite. While he was busy, Karthick quietly made his way to the backyard, stepping toward the familiar wooden table and chairs where they often spent time together.

"Hey, I'm in the backyard, Oldy!" Karthick called out, raising his voice so the old man could hear him from the kitchen.

The old returned with two glasses of plain, fresh grape juice. After Karthick took a sip, the old man asked, "Why are you so angry, Karthick?" Without any hesitation, Karthick blurted out his frustration. "It's just a love poem! Why is she overreacting? I don't get it—why is she so against love? I can't understand her at all. Does reading a love poem make someone fall in love? I don't think so." His words spilled out, filled with confusion and frustration, as he vented to the old man about his mom's reaction.

"Which poet's work upset her so much, Karthick?" the old man asked curiously. "DD's, my favorite," Karthick replied. With a kind smile, the old man nodded. "So, you love reading poems, huh?"

Karthick grinned and eagerly nodded, like an excited child. Suddenly, his eyes lit up with anticipation. "Wait! Where's my birthday present, Oldy?" the old man realized he had completely forgotten to get Karthick a gift and quickly apologized. Karthick, pretending to be upset, smirked and said, "Well, as punishment for forgetting, I want something special. My mom made me mad while I was reading a poem, so now I want you to tell me a love story. That'll be your penalty."

The old looked at Karthick, slightly confused by the request. Karthick's excitement faded as he assumed the old man wouldn't agree. But seeing the disappointment in Karthick's eyes, the old man smiled and said, "Alright, a love story it is!"

It was summer, school and college students had their semester break. Some booked tickets to return to their hometowns, while others planned trips to explore new places and enjoy their holiday.

"Pogathyyy pogathyy ne irunthal nan irupen..." [Don't go, don't go, if you stay, I will stay...] The phone rang on the wooden table in the hall. A chubby young man with curly black hair picked up his Samsung Galaxy S21 and answered, "Hai, Mi! How's it going?" "Yeah, I'm good. Have you had dinner yet, son?" his mom asked. Suddenly, he remembered the chapati still on the pan in the kitchen. In a panic, he quickly ended the call and rushed to the kitchen to save the chapati and turn off the stove. In the kitchen, an old gas stove sat in the center, with utensils stacked on the left. A few water bottles stood nearby, reserved for drinking. Five white ceramic plates were neatly arranged on a stainless-steel rack. Below the sink, a green trashcan was tucked away, while a red trashcan stood by the kitchen door. He rushed to the stove and quickly turned off the gas. Letting out a long breath of relief for saving the chapati, he picked up his phone and called his mom back.

He couldn't get a signal due to the poor network, so he stepped outside and walked to the left. Finally, he got through and said, "Yes, Mi, I'm here." Without missing a beat, she asked, "Why are you making dinner today? What happened to your neighbor who usually cooks for you, we are paying her to cook for you people, aren't we?" He sighed and said, "Wait, Mi, give me a break. She was sick, so she had to go to the hospital. She already let me know and apologized to each of us. Anyway, leave it, Mi. I know why you called. We're getting about twenty-five days off at the end of the semester, and I have some work for the next two days. I'll come home this week, okay?" After his mom said, "Okay," he ended the call, collected his friend's clothes from the drying line, and headed back into the house.

Dev moved from Coimbatore to Kerala to pursue his bachelor's degree. However, hostel life didn't suit him, as he valued personal space and wanted the freedom to explore at night. So, along with two friends from his hometown, he decided to move into a rental house for a more comfortable living arrangement.

Dev called his friends for dinner, having prepared enough for all three of them. "Yeah, coming, dude! I'm starving!" Joseph shouted back. "What about Aryan?" Dev asked. "He went with our neighbor to pick up one of their relatives," Joseph replied. "But Vani said her mom got sick, and they were supposed to go to the hospital," Dev added.

"Yeah, Vani and her mom went to the hospital, and Vasu and his dad went to pick up their relative in Aryan's car," Joseph clarified. "Alright, let's wait for Aryan," Dev suggested. But Joseph's stomach growled loudly in hunger. With a sheepish grin and a laugh, he glanced at Dev, unable to hide his hunger any longer. Dev laughed back and said,

"Alright, let's eat," and the two began their meal together.

A burnt maroon, Honda Jazz car honked from the gate, Dev quickly got up, heading outside with unwashed hands to open it. Without wasting a moment, he told Aryan to hurry and join them for dinner, then returned to his house. Aryan parked the car, handed over the luggage, and went to his place, while Vasu took the bags and headed toward his house.

The girl with brown eyes, dressed in a flowing gown, followed her uncle inside, taking in the surroundings as she stepped through the door. "How many rooms are there, uncle?" she asked, curiously looking around. "There are three rooms," he replied.

Vasu carried her luggage into Vani's room and placed it there, making sure everything was in order.

As Aryan walked into the house, he noticed Joseph and Dev already eating without him. Wanting to stir up some fun, he quickly grabbed a few chapatis from their plates and sprinted to his room, locking the door behind him. Laughing, Joseph and Dev knocked on his door and called out, "Come out Aryan, or we'll lock your door from the outside, and you won't even be able to use the restroom tonight!" They teased him, trying to sound serious but barely holding back their grins.

Aryan, amused, opened the door and burst out laughing. The three of them finally sat down together and resumed their dinner, laughing and enjoying the moment. "I'm missing my family, macha," Aryan said suddenly. Joseph, surprised, asked, "Why, macha? What happened?" Dev glanced at Aryan with curiosity he had never said anything like this before. They had spent the entire two years together, and Aryan had never mentioned missing home.

"Our neighbors, man... their family is so close. Vasu calls his elder sister by her name, and she's so friendly with everyone. She even calls her uncle 'appa.' They're amazing, macha," Aryan explained. "Who's that girl, macha?" Dev asked, intrigued. After thinking for a moment, Aryan replied, "Oh, her name is Darshini. She made me miss my sister."

"Is she cute?" Joseph asked with a flirty grin. Aryan shrugged. "She's alright, but she's a bit tomboyish." Amid the conversation, Dev asked, "So what are you guys planning for the semester holidays?" Joseph answered, "We're staying here. Aryan's family went on a devotional trip, but he didn't want to join them, so he's staying. And I'm not going home this time either. I want to enjoy the break with you guys. Please, macha, stay with us. We only have two semesters left before we finish our degree. Let's make the most of it, all three of us." Joseph looked at Dev, almost pleading, hoping he'd agree to stay with them. "I'll think about it later. Let's eat first," Dev replied, putting the conversation on hold. Among the three, Dev was the most mature, always thoughtful, and composed. Joseph, on the other hand, was the playful one known for his flirty nature. Aryan was a caring and affectionate friend, always looking out for the others.

Vani and her mother returned home, and Vani immediately glanced around the hall, searching for Darshini. It was her first time meeting Darshini in person, though they had spoken on the phone before. Eager and curious, she continued looking until Darshini emerged from the bathroom, freshly showered. Vani jumped up and hugged her tightly, excited to finally meet. After having supper, the two headed to Vani's room.

The house was modest, with a veranda, a hall, a kitchen near the bathroom, and three rooms, all spread across seven hundred square feet. One of the walls in Vani's room was shared with Dev's room, forming a connecting wall between them.

After Dev and his friends washed their hands and grabbed their water bottles, they headed to their rooms. Meanwhile, Vani and Darshini lay on the Pai grass mat, about to relax when a thudding sound came from the door. Vani got up to open the wooden door, and her mother stood there with a request. "Vani, make sure to prepare dosas for the boys next door for tomorrow's breakfast," her mother instructed.

Darshini chimed in, "Chellama, can you make coriander mixer chutney for me too?" With a warm smile, Chellama replied, "Of course, Darshu." After that, they all settled down for the night, drifting off to sleep.

The next morning, as Darshini woke up, Vani entered the room with a cup of coffee. "Sorry, Vani, I don't drink coffee or tea," Darshu said. "Okay, akka," Vani replied with a smile and headed back to the kitchen. After freshening up, Darshu joined her in the kitchen to see what was cooking. Vani was preparing dosas and heating the pan when Darshu offered, "I'll take over, Vani."

"Akka, Mom made your favorite chutney!" Vani said, bringing a big smile to Darshu's face. As Darshu prepared

the dosas, she asked Vani, "Where's Vasu?"

"He went to play football with his friends," Vani replied. Before sitting down to eat, Vani took the breakfast next door to share with the boys. Darshu helped carry the food, and they both headed to the boys' house. The door was already open when they arrived, and Vani called from the doorstep, "Anna!" Joseph responded, "Yeah, Vani, come in and leave the food in the kitchen."

They entered, placing the food on the kitchen counter. As Joseph walked in, he asked, "What's on the menu today?" "Magic dosas, specially made by the great Darshini," Darshu teased with a grin. Joseph was caught off guard and smiled speechlessly. Aryan came out of the bathroom and greeted them with a cheerful, "Good morning!" A bit later, Aryan asked Joseph where Dev was. "He went jogging," Joseph replied.

Darshini then introduced herself, saying hello to both Aryan and Joseph, and asked for their names. They shared their names and hometowns, and Darshini mentioned she was from Chennai.

"Alright, bye for now! I'm starving!" Darshu said with a laugh, and she and Vani returned to their house to have their breakfast.

When Dev returned home, he quietly went to his room and sat down for a while to relax. Meanwhile, Vani locked the main door and sat in the hall.

The next day Darshu, feeling playful, asked Vani, "Shall we play Truth or Dare?" Vani agreed, "Sure!" and began looking for something to spin. "Akka, the black water bottle in our room will be perfect for this," she said with a smile. Excited, they both headed to the room, grabbed the bottle, and quickly started the game. After a while, Vani and Darshu realized it was just the two of them playing, so they began casually asking each other random questions. Darshu asked about Vani's favorite things, and they laughed as they shared stories.

Meanwhile, in the next room, Dev had refreshed and was sitting at his writing desk, trying to focus on a new poem. As he gathered his thoughts, he overheard their conversation through the shared wall.

Vani asked Darshu, "Why don't you drink tea or coffee?" Darshu replied, "I love nature more than anything. That's why I stick to hibiscus tea, traditional Tamil remedies, and healthy foods. Food is an emotion for me. When I have mood swings, I can't eat because I'm not able to enjoy it with the love it deserves."

Hearing her thoughtful answer, Dev couldn't help but smile to himself, appreciating Darshu's unique perspective as he continued to work on his poem. Darshu then asked Vani, "Can you take me to the terrace every night before we go to bed? I love spending time up there in the dark, under the night sky."

In a low voice, Vani quietly said, "Okay." During dinner, Dev and his friends started discussing their plans for the upcoming holidays. Dev agreed to stay with them and had already gotten permission from his mom.

With a grin, Joseph suddenly said, "She's my type." Dev and Aryan exchanged curious glances. Aryan raised an eyebrow and said, "Ohh!" Intrigued, Dev asked, "Who are you talking about?" Aryan chuckled and replied, "He's talking about that girl, Darshu. She came with Vani earlier to bring us breakfast. She chatted with us, no hesitation, none of that girly shyness. That's why Joseph's interested." Dev nodded and said, "Ohh, I see." The group shared a laugh before heading off to bed.

On the other side of the house, Darshu asked Vani if they could go up to the terrace. Vasu, overhearing, laughed and teased Vani, "You know she's afraid of the dark." Darshu's expression fell upon hearing that, and after dinner, she quietly went to her room.

Later that night, Dev walked over to his writing desk, plugging in his phone to charge. The hum of the charger filled the silence as he glanced out of the window, his mind wandering.

Vasu knocked softly on the door. When Darshu opened it, she asked, "What happened, Vasu?" With a playful grin, Vasu said, "Darshu, tomorrow night I'll take you to the terrace." He gave her a quick smile, then turned to leave, saying, "Good night," before disappearing down to his room.

Vani, watching with a possessive look, muttered, "He's never this soft with me, Akka." Darshu chuckled and gently replied, "He's your brother, Vani. Every brother teases his sister it's just how they are. Don't take it to heart. Besides, I'm only staying here for a week, and two days have already passed."

Dev, overhearing the conversation, went to bed with a cloud of confusion. He couldn't shake the thought of Darshu's words "a week." His mind kept circling around it, leaving him restless. He tossed and turned, unable to sleep, as the weight of her short stay lingered in his thoughts.

The next morning, as usual, Dev went for his jog. Chellama and her husband left for work, while Darshu, Vasu, and Vani were getting ready to head out. Meanwhile, Aryan and Joseph had already freshened up and were waiting to have breakfast with Dev. When Dev returned home, he looked troubled and quietly headed to the bathroom for a shower. Meanwhile, Darshu and the others left the house.

Noticing Dev's gloomy expression since the morning, Aryan and Joseph decided to ask him about it during breakfast.

Hearing the sound of the front door, Dev suddenly sprinted towards it, eager to catch a glimpse of Darshu. But by the time he reached the gateway, Darshu and the others had already vanished. Outside, Joseph and Aryan stood watching with puzzled expressions. Aryan, curious, asked Dev why he had rushed out of the house still wrapped in a towel. Without responding, Dev hurried back inside to change. After dressing, he joined them for breakfast, but remained silent, focusing on his food and avoiding eye contact. Joseph and Aryan exchanged glances, waiting for an explanation. Finally, unable to contain his curiosity any longer, Joseph broke the silence and asked, "Dev, what's going on with you this morning?"

Dev closed his eyes, taking a deep, steadying breath. Sensing the weight of the moment, Aryan placed a hand on Joseph's arm and said quietly, "Let's finish our breakfast first, we'll talk later." The three of them ate in silence, the air thick with unspoken questions.

Afterwards, they gathered in Dev's room. Joseph and Aryan sat on the edge of the writing table, their eyes fixed on Dev, who sat in a chair, his fingers tapping lightly on the armrest. The room was still for a few moments, filled only with the faint sound of breathing. Finally, breaking the silence, Dev spoke, his voice low and hesitant. "Macha," he began, his eyes flickering between them, "I think... I have feelings for Darshu."

Aryan's eyes widened in shock, his hand instinctively covering his mouth, while Joseph's eyes grew even bigger, his jaw dropping as he blinked in disbelief, struggling to process what Dev had just confessed. The room, once quiet, now felt charged with emotion as both Aryan and Joseph stared at Dev, unsure of what to say next.

"But how is that possible? You've never acted like this before," Joseph said, still in disbelief. "I don't know," Dev replied, shaking his head. "Yesterday, I overheard Darshu say she's only staying here for a week, and after that, I couldn't sleep at all."

Aryan leaned in, curious. "When did you two talk?" "We didn't," Dev admitted quickly. "I overheard her talking with Vani last night. They didn't know I was listening. You see, from this writing table, we can hear everything happening in the other room, but they can't hear us. There's always some noise on their side, but in my room, it's quiet. So, whatever's said over there, I can pick up easily, but they have no idea."

"What made you fall for her?" Aryan asked, his curiosity evident. "I haven't even seen her face yet," Dev admitted, his voice softer. "It's strange, but just hearing her talk through the wall her thoughts, the way she speaks it made me curious about her. I wanted to know more. That's why I've been trying to see her. I made two attempts today was the second one, as you saw this morning."

The three of them fell into a deep silence, each lost in thought. After a while, Aryan let out a sigh and said, "I'll help you." Joseph, blinking as if he had just pieced something together, nodded and added, "Alright, I've got an idea. Tomorrow, I'm heading out with a friend from college, so Dev, you should stay home in the morning and skip your jog."

Aryan's eyes lit up. "That's perfect! Since Darshu and Vani have been bringing breakfast over, if you're home, you'll have a chance to finally meet her." Dev's face brightened with excitement. "Thanks, guys!"

With the plan set, they each returned to their daily routine.

Vani, Vasu, and Darshu returned home in the evening, worn out from the day. Exhausted, the entire family decided to have supper earlier than usual. While the three gathered in Vani's room for some quiet conversation, on the other hand in the next wall, Dev, Joseph, and Aryan, curious to hear their discussion, silently ate their meal at the writing table in Dev's room, trying not to miss a word.

"I'm sorry, Darshu," Vasu said, his voice heavy with fatigue. "I promised to take you to the terrace tonight, but

I'm just too tired. Can we go tomorrow?"

Darshu smiled and reassured him, "No problem at all." Then, with a curious glint in her eyes, she asked, "By the way, did you both like what I bought for you today?"

Vani and Vasu exchanged a quick glance before nodding enthusiastically. "We loved it!" they chimed in unison.

Vani, feeling a little curious, leaned forward. "Darshu, ever since you got here, you haven't seemed eager to go out much. You've just stayed home, not even looking bored. How do you do it?"

With a soft smile, Darshu explained, "If I wanted to go shopping or see the beach, I could do that anytime back in Chennai. But here, surrounded by nature and the calm of this place, I find peace. I'm really enjoying the quiet and spending time with you all."

From the other room, Dev and his friends overheard her words, and they couldn't help but smile, nodding in agreement with her sentiment.

As the night wore on, Vasu let out a long yawn. "I'm too tired to go back to my room. I think I'll sleep here tonight, if that's okay." Vani and Darshu smiled knowingly, and soon, the three of them, heavy with sleep, drifted off into peaceful slumber.

After washing their hands, Dev, Joseph, and Aryan moved to Joseph's room. Joseph glanced at Dev and teased, "I think you're drawn to her more for her character than anything else."

Aryan said, "Whatever the reason, it's clear Dev's starting to like her. So, it's only right that we help him out." After sharing a knowing laugh, the trio wrapped up their conversation and headed to their own rooms for the night.

The next morning, before Dev and Aryan had even woken up, Joseph slipped out early to meet a friend. Once Dev and Aryan were up and refreshed, they found themselves anxiously watching the clock, waiting for Darshu and Vani to bring breakfast. Dev, growing restless, walked toward the main door, pacing the hallway with nervous, while Aryan, laughing in the hall, couldn't help but laugh at his friend's anxious behavior.

Just then, the doorbell rang. Dev, startled, rushed to open it. As the door swung open, Vani stepped inside with a bright smile. Dev, with a mix of excitement and hesitation, peeked over her back, hoping to see Darshu standing behind her. But to his dismay, it was Vasu, not Darshu, who followed Vani, carrying breakfast and lunch in hand. Dev's face fell slightly as Aryan stifled a laugh from the hall.

Dev sighed in frustration and subtly raised his eyebrows at Aryan, signaling him to ask Vani why Darshu hadn't come. Being mature yet shy, Dev was never particularly close with Vani or Vasu, so he stood awkwardly by the door, avoiding direct conversation.

Noticing Dev's unusual behavior, Vani leaned toward Aryan and asked in a whisper, "Why is Dev acting so weird? And why did he skip his morning jog?" With a mischievous grin, Aryan quickly covered for his friend. "Oh, he's got some leg pain, so no jog today," he said casually. Then, with a playful nudge, Aryan asked, "By the way, since Darshu's been here, she's always helped you bring food. Why didn't she come with you today?"

Vani, unaware of the tension in the room, replied matter-of-factly, "She's leaving the day after tomorrow and has already booked her return ticket. She's busy packing her clothes, so she couldn't come."

Hearing this, Dev's heart sank. Without saying a word, he turned and walked to his room, locking the door behind him with a loud door sound.

Aryan had taken the car to the service center earlier that morning. With their trip planned for the following week, he was eager to get everything in order. However, at the showroom, he was informed that due to the weekend, the car wouldn't be ready for another three days. Disappointed but understanding, Aryan returned home, intending to chat with Dev about the delay.

However, when he got back, he found Dev still holed up in his room, refusing to open the door since morning. Aryan knocked a few times, but Dev didn't respond. He decided to give him some space, hoping Dev would come around by evening. Later that day, Joseph returned home, brimming with excitement. Spotting Aryan, he immediately asked, "What happened this morning? How did things go?" Aryan explained the situation, telling him about the car delay and how Dev had locked himself away in his room since hearing about Darshu's upcoming departure.

With a determined look, Joseph said, "We need to talk to him." They both headed to Dev's room and eventually convinced him to come out. Leading him to Joseph's room,

Joseph offered Dev some words of encouragement. "You still have a chance; Dev. Darshu is going to the terrace tonight. You can see her there, no need to worry so much."

After some persuasion, Dev finally felt a bit reassured. That night, he went up to the terrace early, hoping to calm his nerves before Darshu and Vasu arrived.

Meanwhile, outside the house, Vasu called out to Darshu with a cheerful tone, prompting her to step outside with a bright smile on her face. Joseph and Aryan, standing discreetly outside, watched as Darshu headed upstairs. Once they confirmed she was indeed going to the terrace, they exchanged satisfied glances and went back inside the house, grinning broadly, knowing the stage was set for Dev to finally have his moment.

Hearing the soft sound of footsteps approaching, Dev's heart raced. Quickly, he rushed over to the washing stone, casually sitting down and reclining to the side, trying to make it seem as though he was just relaxing there, as if it were a natural, everyday moment. Moments later, Vasu and Darshu stepped onto the terrace.

Karthick's mom felt a heavy weight on her heart as she worked in the kitchen, regretful over having scolded him earlier that afternoon. The guilt made it hard for her to focus on even the simplest tasks. Hesitant but unable to bear the unease, she decided to call him. When his ringtone echoed from his room, she realized with frustration that he had left his phone behind.

Anxious, she hurried outside, searching for him. With hope in her heart, she crossed the road and thought of checking at the old man's house nearby. Upon seeing his shoes left outside the door, she breathed a sigh of relief, knowing he was there. Not wanting to disturb him, she quietly turned around and headed back home, feeling slightly more at ease.

Dev stretched his back, eagerly watching for their arrival, his fingers drumming nervously. Vasu and Darshu paused on the second floor to catch their breath, knowing they had one more flight of stairs before reaching the terrace. Just a few steps away from the next landing, the power went out. Feeling a surge of tension, Vasu urged Darshu to turn on her phone's flashlight, only to realize she hadn't brought her phone along, wanting to fully enjoy the terrace time. Taking a deep breath, Vasu pressed forward. When they finally reached the terrace, Darshu and Vasu exchanged relieved glances and sighed they had made it.

Dev turned back quickly, hoping to catch a glimpse of her face, but the closed terrace and power outage allowed him only to see the form of the person not a clear vision on them. Disappointed, he sat quietly, not wanting them to know he was there. Darshu and Vasu made their way to the corner near the washing stone. Darshu, her eyes gleaming, was captivated by the beauty of the crescent moon on its third night, sinking into the peaceful silence of the moment.

Vasu broke the quiet. "Darshu, Vani's scared of the dark. You're a girl like her, but you seem to enjoy it. Why?" With a soft, knowing smile, Darshu replied, "Those who understand that the silence of darkness holds the key to peace will never fear it." "Ohh," Vasu responded thoughtfully and began to walk away.

Dev shifted slightly, trying once more to see her face, but Darshu's loose hair fell in a way that kept her hidden from him. Meanwhile, Vasu felt someone calling his name. Moving closer to the terrace door, he focused and recognized his father's voice, asking them to come downstairs due to the power cut. Vasu relayed the message to Darshu and told her to join him.

After a few minutes, Dev quietly moved down the stairs. Aryan and Joseph were waiting eagerly, hoping to hear if he had seen her, but Dev brushed crossed them and went straight to his room. They followed him to the doorstep but didn't enter, exchanging glances as they realized he was upset. Although the door wasn't locked, they silently retreated to their own rooms.

The next morning, Joseph couldn't wait any longer for Aryan to wake up. Impatient, he nudged Aryan awake and dragged him to Dev's door. Aryan reached out to knock, but the door swung open on its own. Joseph leaned forward, peeking inside. They found Dev slumped over his writing table, fast asleep. With a shared look of concern, they quietly stepped inside, sensing the depth of Dev's sadness.

As they approached, Aryan's eyes fell on Dev's open diary. In the curiosity, he picked it up. Joseph moved closer, joining him. Both stared at the pages, realizing Dev had spent the entire night writing. Without a word, Joseph began reading the poem softly, his lips moving without sounding.

She concealed her face,

Even with my breath, just a whisper away,

Yet still, my heart fell silently.

Her voice, Unknown, tied me tight,

In the whisper, I found my light.

I yearned to feel her aura near,

Her melody voice is the only thing I hear.

I set my heart upon the wall,

Like a gentle breeze that makes my heart skip a beat.

Though I've never seen her face,

Her voice alone fills the void, a sweet serenade in every space.

Joseph and Aryan stepped out of Dev's room, quietly closing the door behind them. They made their way up to the terrace to talk. On the terrace, Joseph stood in silence, struggling to express his thoughts. Aryan broke the tension, saying, "Dev's serious about Darshu." Joseph turned to Aryan, his expression puzzled. "I don't get it, macha. I've never seen Dev like this. I'm usually the one who's into girls, talking about them all the time. Dev's always acted so mature, but now he's fallen for Darshu just by hearing her voice and knowing her personality. I still can't believe it."

Just then, an old man, dressed in a brown vest and lungi, appeared on the terrace. Aryan muttered, "The house owner is here, Jo. Let's go." They both forced a polite smile and quickly headed back downstairs.

The next day, after lunch, Vani and Darshu entered the room together. Since it was Sunday, the whole family had eaten lunch together. Chellama came into Vani's room carrying two glasses of wheat payesh. As she handed her right-hand payesh to Darshu, Darshu flopped onto the bed, groaning, "Chellama, I'm already so full, I can barely move. Please, I can't eat anymore!"

Chellama smiled at Darshu and teased, "Okay, don't act like a child, haha!" Vani happily enjoyed the payesh. Later, Vasu stepped into the room and rested his head on Vani's lap. He gave Chellama a playful look, realizing she hadn't brought him the payesh. But then, with a grin, Darshu revealed that she had taken the payesh from Chellama, the one meant for her, and handed it to him. With a long face, Chellama sighed, "By this time tomorrow, Darshu will be on the train." Vasu and Vani stopped drinking payesh and their expressions fell, and Vasu quietly left the room.

Joseph and Aryan stood near the clothesline, discussing how to arrange for Dev to meet Darshu before she left the next day. Just then, Vasu came out looking glum. After freshening up, Dev searched for Joseph and Aryan and heard their voices outside. He stepped out to join them. As Vasu approached, Joseph and Aryan quickly shifted the conversation to the weather. Dev soon joined them, and Aryan, noticing Vasu's gloomy expression, nudged Joseph to take a look. Sensing something was off, Dev asked, "What's wrong, Vasu?" Vasu then shared the news of Darshu's departure and her train schedule for the next day. Joseph and Aryan exchanged knowing grins, and Dev quickly caught on, without asking Vasu revealed Darshu's travel plans.

A raindrop fell on Vasu's face. He glanced up and realized it was about to rain, so he quickly grabbed all the clothes from the line and dashed back to the house. Dev and his friends did the same, gathering their clothes and heading inside. Later that night, Chellama asked Vani to take supper over to the boys' house. Struggling to carry the heavy vessel, Vani was relieved when Darshu offered to help. But Chellama intervened, saying, "It's alright, Darshu. Vasu will take it with her." Darshu, catching the hint, handed the vessel to Vasu. With some confusion, Vani delivered the food to the boys.

When Vani returned home, she found her father and the rest of the family discussing tomorrow's plans. Chellama and Vani's father apologized to Darshu, explaining they wouldn't be able to take the day off to see her off. Darshu assured them it was no trouble and promised she won't tell her parents. Vasu also told, he would take care of everything the next day. What the boys' next door didn't know was that Darshu's uncle and aunt wouldn't be there to see her off either.

The next morning, after breakfast, Aryan and Dev went to Joseph's room to bring him outside to wait for Darshu. As they entered, they noticed Joseph scribbling something on a piece of paper. Aryan quietly stepped behind him to peek at what he was writing. Suddenly, with a grin, Joseph declared, "It's affection, not love!" Aryan bursting into laughter. Dev glanced at Aryan with confusion. Dev asked, "Why are you both acting so strange?" grinned and replied, "Macha, Jo scribbled FLAMES for you and Darshu." Dev's expression darkened, and he walked out, with Aryan and Joseph following close behind. The three of them stood by the hibiscus plant. With a tense look, Dev said, "In twenty minutes, they'll all come out to send her off."

Joseph shrugged and said, "Okay, but why are we standing here so early?" Aryan quickly responded, "Chellama auntie is too sharp. If we come out the same time they do, she'll catch on to why we're here." Joseph raised his eyebrows and exclaimed, "Ohhh, makes sense!" Just then, they heard a noise from inside a house nearby. Rushing over, they found an elderly man collapsed in pain. Aryan helped him to his feet, while Dev gathered the scattered wooden items and moved them to the corner of the hall. Joseph fetched water for the man and asked, "What happened, uncle?" Aryan helped him settle into a wooden armchair, while Dev set the glass on the table. The house owner winced and explained, "I was trying to move some wood from the attic when I slipped and fell."

As they finished helping him, Aryan heard a sound from outside, and Dev, realizing what it was, sprinted toward the gate. Vani locked the door and headed for the entrance, as Dev and his friends dashed toward the gateway. By the time they arrived, Darshu was already stepping into the auto. Dev, breathing heavily, bent over with his hands on his knees. His eyes locked on the handlebar of the auto, where he noticed a delicate hand adorned with a heart-shaped ring on the finger. A heavy feeling sank into his chest.

Aryan and Joseph stood beside him, unsure of how to console their friend. As the auto turned the corner at the end of the street, Dev's phone rang. The familiar tune echoed: "Pogathey, pogathey... ne irunthal naan irupen." [Don't go, don't go... if you stay, I'll stay.]

Dev stood frozen, his heart heavy, as a single tear rolled down his left cheek.

An ant crawled out of the glass. The clouds were tinged with a soft candy pink, and birds were returning to their nests. Karthick sat frozen, lost in thought. The old man let out a deep breath and picked up the juice glasses from the table. He gently shook Karthick's shoulder and said, "Come on, young man, let's head inside. It's getting late."

But Karthick was still caught up in the story of Dev and Darshu's love, moving slowly toward the house. As he reached the hallway, he heard the old man's voice from the bedroom. Standing outside, Karthick called out, "What is it, Oldy?" The old man replied, "Come in, Karthick, I've got something for you."

Entering the room for the first time, Karthick looked around, curious and excited. As the old man pulled out a copy of the book 'Susurration of a Hidden Soul', Karthick's eyes froze on a picture hanging on the wall. It was of a girl's hand, wearing a heart-shaped ring, gripping the handlebar of an auto. Below the image, the words "Deva and Darshini" were inscribed. Karthick stood motionless, the weight of the moment sinking in.

CHAPTER SIX

When Time Stood Still

-By Jeffrin Matthew. M. R

It was a beautiful morning. I woke up early today, the kind of early where the world still feels half-asleep, wrapped in the soft glow of dawn. I made myself a cup of coffee, the aroma filling the kitchen as I watched the steam rise, swirling lazily like the thoughts in my mind. Today felt different, though I couldn't yet put my finger on why." With the warm mug cradled in my hands, I stepped out onto the balcony, letting the cool morning air greet me.

The world outside was just waking up, bathed in soft shades of gold and pink. I took a sip of my coffee, the rich, earthy flavor grounding me as I gazed out at the trees swaying gently in the breeze. Birds flitted between branches, their songs mingling with the distant hum of the city, creating a melody that was both familiar and comforting. As I stood there, I felt a quiet contentment—a connection to the simple beauty of the morning. The sky, painted with the first light of day, seemed to hold endless possibilities. It was in moments like these that I felt the world slow down, allowing me to simply be, to breathe, and to appreciate the tranquillity that nature offered. I had come here for my vacation, seeking refuge in this secluded house near the shore. The gentle sound of waves lapping against the shore was a constant companion, soothing and rhythmic, as if the ocean itself was breathing. From the balcony, I could see the expanse of the sea stretching out to meet the horizon, where the sky kissed the water in a blur of blues and golds. This place was everything I needed it to be—quiet, serene, and far from the rush of my usual life.

The house, with its weathered wooden beams and large windows, felt like a sanctuary, a place where time seemed to slow down. Here, the days were marked by the changing tides, and the nights by the sound of the sea whispering through the open windows. As I stood there, sipping my coffee, I felt a sense of calm wash over me, the kind that only comes when you're truly at peace with where you are. I had no plans for the day, no agenda to follow. This vacation was a gift to myself, a chance to reconnect with the things that truly mattered—nature, solitude, and the quiet joy of simply being. I finished the last sip of my coffee, feeling its warmth still lingering as I set the empty mug on the balcony's rail. Reluctantly, I turned back inside, the stillness of the house greeting me as I stepped into the kitchen.

The peacefulness of the morning was still fresh in my mind, but just as I reached for the sink, my foot caught on something—a chair leg, maybe, or the uneven edge of the floor. Before I could react, I stumbled hard, my hands grasping at the counter for balance. A sharp pain shot through my knee as I hit the ground, and for a moment, everything around me seemed to spin. I lay there, dazed, the quiet morning suddenly shattered by the harsh reality of the fall. My breath came in shallow gasps as I tried to steady myself, the calm of the morning replaced by a sudden rush of adrenaline. I felt a wave of dizziness wash over me as I lay on the cold kitchen floor. My vision blurred, the edges of the room swirling as if the ground itself was shifting beneath me. The pain in my knee dulled, overtaken by the strange light-headedness' that followed the fall. Before I could fully grasp what was happening, everything went dark. It was only a few seconds, but it felt like I'd been submerged in a deep, heavy silence—no sounds, no thoughts, just a vast emptiness. When I finally came to, the world slowly returned in pieces. The soft hum of the fridge. The sunlight spilled through the window. I blinked, disoriented, still lying on the floor, trying to make sense of what just happened. Had I fainted? My body felt heavy, like I was waking from a long, deep sleep, even though I knew I had only been out for a moment. Shakily, I propped myself up, my heart racing as I tried to catch my breath. Something about the experience left a strange sense of unease lingering in my chest. When I opened my eyes again, I wasn't on the cold kitchen floor anymore. I was lying in a bed, the unfamiliar sheets soft beneath me. Confused, I blinked a few times, trying to shake the fog from my mind.

My head still felt heavy, and for a moment, I wondered if I was dreaming. Then, I noticed her. A girl, standing quietly beside the bed. Her expression was calm, almost serene, but her presence was unsettling in its strangeness. I didn't know her, and yet, there was something familiar about the way she stood, like she belonged here, beside me, waiting. 'Who... are you?' I managed to ask; my voice hoarse. She didn't answer right away, only watching me with a curious intensity, as though she was trying to decide how much to tell me. As I lay there, the question of how I ended up in this bed gnawed at me. Had she found me after the fall? Or had something stranger occurred? As my eyes focused, I saw her more clearly. She was, without question, the most beautiful woman I had ever met. Her features were delicate, almost ethereal, like something out of a dream. Her eyes, deep and unwavering, held a calm that made me forget, just for a moment, the strangeness of waking up here. She stood there, quiet and composed, her long hair cascading over her shoulders, catching the soft light that filtered through the curtains.

There was something timeless about her, something that made the rest of the room seem to blur around her presence. I couldn't place it, but I felt as though I had known her, or at least dreamed of her, in some faraway moment I couldn't quite recall. 'Who are you?' I asked again, this time with more urgency, my heart racing, though I couldn't say if it was from fear or fascination. She still didn't answer right away, but the way she looked at me—like she was searching for something in my eyes—made me feel that her silence held more meaning than words could offer. I fell in love with her in no time. It wasn't the kind of slow, blossoming feeling I'd experienced before. This was different—instant, intense, like I had been waiting my whole life for this one moment.

There was something in the way she looked at me, the way her gaze lingered just a little longer, that made me believe she felt it too. It wasn't just admiration. It was recognition. Her presence calmed me, made the confusion and disorientation from before slip into the background. I should have been asking questions—how I got here, who she was—but none of that seemed to matter. In that moment, it was as if the world had shrunk down to just the two of us, and the silence between us felt like an unspoken agreement, a bond that had formed without a single word exchanged. She smiled then, a soft, knowing smile that made my heart race. It was as though she could see right through me, into my very thoughts, and I was certain she knew. She must have felt it too—this strange, undeniable pull between us. It was too strong, too immediate to be one-sided. As she handed me a glass of water, I couldn't take my eyes off her. The simple gesture felt intimate, like an unspoken promise. I took a sip, and immediately, I noticed something. The water—it tasted different, sweeter than anything I had ever drunk before. It was refreshing, but more than that, it felt... alive. I couldn't explain it, but it was as if with every sip, I felt more connected to her, to this place, and yet I wanted to take her with me, back to the life I had left behind.

'Come with me,' I said, surprising even myself with the suddenness of the request. The words tumbled out before I had a chance to think them through. 'To the city, where I live. I don't want to leave you here.'She didn't seem startled by my words. In fact, she smiled again—that soft, knowing smile that had already begun to feel familiar. She stepped closer, her hand brushing against mine as she handed me the water, and for a moment, I thought she might say yes without hesitation. There was something in her eyes, a shared understanding that what was happening between us was real, powerful, and immediate. I couldn't explain why, but I wanted her to be a part of my life, away from this quiet shore and strange house. I imagined us walking through the busy streets, her by my side, as though we were always meant to be. But as I waited for her answer, part of me wondered—was she even from this world? This place already felt like a dream, and yet everything about her felt more real than anything I had ever known. She gently said, 'Shall we go now, or should we wait till the vacation is over?' Her voice was soft, almost musical, and the question hung in the air between us, light and unpressured. It was as if she had already decided she would come with me, but was offering me the choice, as though she understood I wasn't just asking for company—I was asking her to step into my world. For a moment, I was speechless. The calm acceptance in her words, the way she had so easily embraced the idea of leaving with me, was unlike anything I had expected. No hesitation. No questions. It felt as if she had been waiting for me, as if the idea of us leaving together was always meant to happen.

'Now,' I said almost too quickly, my heart racing at the thought of her beside me, back in my city, back in my life. The idea of waiting felt unbearable, like each passing minute without her in my world would be wasted time. But as soon as I said it, doubt crept in. This place, this strange and beautiful house by the shore, had its own magic, a quiet stillness that felt almost otherworldly. What if leaving broke whatever spell had brought us together? What if the connection we shared was tied to this place, this moment? She seemed to read my hesitation, her eyes softening as she watched me struggle between impulse and thought. 'We have time,' she said, her voice steady. 'The city will wait for us, and so will I.' There was no rush in her words, just the gentle assurance that whether we left now or later, we would leave together.

We left the house by the shore that same day, the sound of the waves fading behind us as we drove back to the city. It felt surreal, taking her with me—this woman who seemed almost like a dream herself. But as we merged onto busy streets and passed the familiar sights of my everyday life, nothing about her seemed out of place. She belonged with me, and I with her. The days turned into months, and the months into years. We built a life together, the two of us weaving our own routines and memories into the fabric of the bustling city. Though the magic of that shore still lingered in my mind, she brought a new kind of magic into my world—a magic that existed in the ordinary, in the small moments we shared. The way her laughter filled the room, or the quiet comfort of her presence on a rainy afternoon. We didn't rush. We spent years growing together, understanding each other in ways that words could never explain. It was as if we had known each other forever, yet still discovered something new with every passing day. And then, one day, I knew. The time had come to make her not just a part of my life, but my life itself.

We married in a small ceremony, surrounded by the people who had become our family. The vows we exchanged felt almost unnecessary, as though we had made those promises to each other long ago, back on that shore where our story first began. As I looked at her, standing across from me in her simple white dress, I couldn't help but think back to that first morning when I had woken up to find her beside me. It had felt like a dream then, but now, with her hand in mine and the weight of the years we had spent together, I knew it was more real than anything I'd ever experienced. She was my reality, my forever.

Ten years had passed since the day we first met, and yet it felt like both an instant and a lifetime. From that strange, magical morning by the shore to the day we stood side by side, saying our vows, every moment felt woven together into one continuous story. Time hadn't taken away the awe I felt for her; if anything, it deepened my love, grounding it in the reality of the life we had built. I often thought back to that moment when I first opened my eyes and saw her standing beside me, not knowing then how much she would come to mean to me. I had fallen in love with her so quickly, and now, after ten years, I realised I had only just begun to understand the depth of that love.

Our marriage hadn't changed much between us. It was more like a natural progression, a formal recognition of what we both already knew—that we were meant to be together. Those ten years had been full of laughter, quiet mornings, small arguments that ended in smiles, and the shared silence that only two people who truly understand each other can enjoy. I'd sometimes catch her looking at me with the same soft, knowing smile she had on that very first day, and it never failed to make my heart skip.

She still had that quiet magic about her, the same aura that made me feel like I was the luckiest person in the world to have found her. Ten years had passed, and yet, standing next to her, it felt like no time at all. Our journey was far from over, and as we looked to the future, I couldn't help but feel that the best was still to come. She gifted me with two beautiful boys, and with their arrival, our world grew even richer. I remember the first time I held each of them, small and fragile, yet filled with so much life. It was in those moments that I realized how love could expand—how my heart could make room for so much more. She had already transformed my life, and now, with these two boys, she had given me the gift of a family.

As the years passed, I watched them grow older each day, their laughter filling our home, their energy a constant reminder of how quickly time moved. They had her eyes, her quiet strength, and I often marvelled at how much of her I saw in them—the way they looked at the world with curiosity, with wonder. Every day felt like an adventure, watching them discover new things, while we learned more about ourselves as parents. Our family grew stronger, our bond deepening with every milestone, every challenge, and every quiet moment we shared. Dinners at the table, messy mornings filled with chaos and laughter, the simple joy of a weekend spent together—it all became the fabric of our lives. And through it all, the love that had first drawn me to her never faded. In fact, it only grew, enriched by the life we had built together. She and I remained as connected as ever, our bond now stretched to include the two boys who had become the center of our world. It wasn't just the love between the two of us anymore—it was the love we had created, shared, and nurtured in our children. And with each passing day, as our sons grew older and our family stronger, I knew that this was the life I had always dreamed of, even before I knew it was possible. As the years continued to slip by, my boys grew older, and soon enough, they reached the age when love began to take on a new meaning for them. It wasn't just a phase or a fleeting emotion; it was something deep and profound.

My firstborn, with his bright smile and adventurous spirit, fell in love and decided it was time to take that next step. I remember the day he came to us, nervous yet excited, his eyes gleaming with hope. He told us about the girl who had captured his heart—someone he had met during college, someone who understood him in a way that left him breathless. He spoke of her with such admiration and respect that I could see the love radiating from him. I exchanged glances with my wife, and I could tell we both felt the same way: pride mixed with a twinge of nostalgia. 'If she makes you happy, then we accept your decision,' I said, my voice steady, though my heart swelled with emotion. It was a bittersweet moment, knowing that our boy was stepping into a new chapter of his life, but the joy in his eyes reassured me that he was ready. My wife smiled warmly, her support echoing mine, and together we welcomed his choice with open arms.

The wedding planning began, filled with laughter and anticipation. Our home buzzed with excitement as we helped him and his fiancée prepare for their big day. It was a beautiful celebration, marked by love and joy, surrounded by family and friends. I watched as my son stood there, radiating happiness, and my heart swelled with pride. He was becoming a man, ready to start a family of his own. As I stood next to my wife, we shared knowing smiles, a silent acknowledgment of how far we had come. Watching our son marry the girl he loved felt like a circle completing itself—our love had created a foundation, and now he was building his own. We accepted this new chapter wholeheartedly, embracing the changes while cherishing the memories we had built as a family. A couple of years later, my other boy approached me with the same mix of excitement and nervousness that his brother had displayed not too long before. He stood before me, his hands clasped together, and a hopeful glimmer in his eyes. 'Dad, I've found someone special,' he said, a grin spreading across his face. 'I want to marry her. 'I felt a wave of pride wash over me.

Just like his brother, he had found love, and it was clear from the way he spoke that this was serious. I nodded, smiling as I embraced him. 'If she makes you happy, son, we fully support you.' His face lit up, and it was clear he felt the same thrill of happiness that had filled our home during the first wedding. Her parents soon visited our house for a meeting, a customary gesture to bring our families together before the union of their children. As we prepared for their arrival, my wife and I busied ourselves, wanting everything to be perfect. When the doorbell rang, I could feel the electricity in the air. Her parents were warm and welcoming, their smiles reflecting the same joy we felt. We exchanged pleasantries, laughter filling the living room as we shared stories about our children, our eyes sparkling with pride at the mention of their accomplishments and dreams. My wife and I watched as our son and his fiancée interacted, their chemistry undeniable, making us feel that this union was destined. After a delightful dinner filled with laughter and heartfelt conversations, we gathered in the living room for a moment that felt almost sacred. My son took her hand, and I could see the love between them in the way they looked at each other. Their shared excitement for the future was palpable. With her parents beside us, we formed a circle, a family in the making.

'To new beginnings,' I said, raising my glass, and everyone joined in, echoing the sentiment. We toasted to love, unity, and the blossoming relationship between our families. That night, I felt a sense of completeness, knowing that our family was expanding in the most beautiful way possible. The two new buds of love were ready to bloom, and I couldn't wait to see the life they would build together. After my younger son got married, the house was filled with a vibrant energy that lingered in the air, echoing the love and laughter shared throughout the day. The ceremony had been beautiful, filled with heartfelt vows and joyful celebrations that united not just two individuals, but two families. As I looked around, I saw the faces of loved ones—friends, family, and everyone who had supported our boys through their journeys. It was a moment of pure happiness, and I felt incredibly grateful.

That night, as I lay in bed beside my wife, the warmth of the day wrapped around us like a comforting blanket. My heart was full, and I felt a deep sense of contentment wash over me. The celebrations, the laughter, and the love that filled our home left me feeling lighter than air. I reflected on how far we had come, how our family had grown, and how much joy it had brought to our lives.

With everything settled, I closed my eyes and sank into the softness of the pillows, feeling an overwhelming sense of peace. It was the best sleep of my life—deeper and more restorative than I had ever experienced. As I drifted off, I allowed myself to dream of the future, filled with possibilities and new memories yet to be made. I envisioned my boys finding their paths, building their families, and sharing their lives with the partners they loved.

In that quiet moment, I realized that the love my wife and I had nurtured had blossomed into something beautiful, stretching out to encompass our children and their futures. It was a legacy of love, one that I hoped would continue to grow. I surrendered to the comforting embrace of sleep, knowing that tomorrow would bring more joy, more laughter, and more love.

However, just as I began to drift into that blissful slumber, an unexpected pain shot through my head, jolting me back to consciousness. It was a dull ache, persistent and annoying, and I instinctively reached up to massage my temples. As I did, I felt another discomfort—a nagging pain in my knee that seemed to throb in time with my heartbeat.

I tried to brush it off, attributing the sensations to the long, emotionally charged day we had just experienced. Weddings had a way of draining energy, I thought, even amidst the joy and celebration. But as I shifted in bed, the discomfort refused to fade. I felt a wave of concern wash over me, juxtaposed with the warm glow of happiness I had just felt.

'Are you alright?' my wife asked, her voice laced with concern as she turned to me, noticing my sudden stillness. 'I'm fine,' I replied, forcing a smile, but the pain lingered, casting a shadow over my blissful thoughts. I didn't want to ruin the moment, didn't want to shift our focus away from the joy of the day. Yet, there was a nagging feeling that something wasn't quite right. As I lay there, staring at the ceiling, I couldn't shake the unease growing inside me.

I took a deep breath, trying to relax, reminding myself that tomorrow was a new day, filled with potential and love. But the pain persisted, a reminder that even in our happiest moments, life had a way of throwing unexpected challenges our way. I hoped it would pass soon so I could enjoy the bliss of my family and the memories we had just created. As I turned to my side, I felt my wife's hand reach out, resting gently on my shoulder, her touch grounding me as I fought to find my way back to that peaceful sleep. 'Let's talk about it in the morning,' she said softly, and I nodded, grateful for her presence. I closed my eyes again, hoping that sleep would take me back to a place of joy, where the pains of the day could not reach me.

But the pain didn't go away. It intensified, pulling me from the gentle embrace of sleep, and I opened my eyes, blinking against the sudden light. As my vision cleared, confusion washed over me. I wasn't in my comfortable bed beside my wife; instead, I found myself lying on the ground in a dimly lit room that felt hauntingly familiar. The memories flooded back, and a sense of dread filled me.

I struggled to sit up, my knee still aching from the fall. The memories of an entire lifetime flashed through my mind in rapid succession—meeting the woman of my dreams, building a life, watching my sons grow, their marriages, the love that had filled every corner of my world. But now, everything felt surreal, like a movie played too fast and too bright.

I glanced around and realized I was still in the house by the shore, the same place where I had started my vacation. The same morning sun spilled through the windows, casting long shadows on the floor where I had stumbled. It hadn't been 40 years. It had barely been 40 minutes. A sense of loss and confusion washed over me. How could it have felt so real? The touch of my wife's hand, the sound of my sons' laughter, the joy of watching their lives unfold—it had all been so vivid, so complete. I sat there, breathing heavily, trying to reconcile the life I had lived in my mind with the reality before me.

'Was it all a dream?' I whispered, my voice trembling with disbelief. But deep down, I knew it was. The fall had knocked me unconscious, and in that brief moment, my mind had created an entire world—decades of love and life. I reached up and touched my forehead, still throbbing from the impact. The pain was real enough, but the life I had lived? That was gone, dissolving into nothing more than a fleeting dream. I felt the weight of the emptiness that came with the realization as if I had lost something precious, something I would never truly have.

Standing up, I glanced outside the window. The ocean waves crashed rhythmically against the shore as if nothing had changed. The world was exactly as it had been before I fell, untouched by the passage of those imagined years. Yet, in my heart, I carried the memory of those 40 years. They may have been a dream, but they had shaped me in ways I couldn't explain. The love, the family—it had felt real. And maybe, in some strange way, it was."

CHAPTER SEVEN

A Voyage in Pursuit of Life's Destiny

-By Paul Gabriel. C

1. Braiding words through wandering Gaze.

The golden light from the big orangish-red ball brightened the day and bathed everything around us, the title was on the line, and the background sound made by my mates gave me a different level of confidence amid heavy pressure. Every sweat gland in my body busted open and I was drenched in sweat as I was competing in the final round of inter-college badminton games. Every point made by my opponent and me drove the crowd mad. A new set of vibes was created, and everybody around us started throwing out their ideas. If something went wrong, they began to shout and scream at both of us which put lots of pressure on my shoulders. As the due (score) was twenty, for a moment I almost had the upper hand on that game. As the shuttlecock soared high with the powerful smash from the hands of Prem which hurtled towards my court in no time, I couldn't make it and again the due was changed to twenty-one. Both of us were twenty all, as the crowd erupted in cheer for Prem. Now, it was my turn to get my payback. So, I brushed myself off, got a towel from my mate, and dried my hands as I was fully drenched in sweat. The game continued for five more minutes, both of us moving very carefully and I was trying to place the shuttlecock in the best possible way I could. It was intense and everybody around the ground gathered surrounding the court, with the back-to-back powerful smash on perfect timing made it possible for me to do what I thought moments ago. The atmosphere was charged with pride and excitement with the overwhelmed joy I jumped off and punched the air with my bat on the other hand. My mates and the crowd lifted me onto their shoulders, and that was a day I will always cherish. Me and my boys Ephi, Suki, Matthew, and the rest of us had lots of fun among us. Prem and I had a little chat and he threw me a challenge to face him on the next Sunday eve in the Anna stadium court. It was a very good thing to have an opponent like Prem. I replied to him "If you want that to happen, then you are my brother". After a nail-biting game, we shook hands which was true sportsmanship.

As the stage was being set for the awards ceremony, anticipation filled the air. The boys and I did some arrangement work on the stage and the other pieces of stuff. The ceremony started upon the arrival of our principal Sir and the secretary on a white Honda City. As the ceremony started the crowd buzzed with excitement, eagerly awaiting the announcement of the overall championship winners. When the Department of History was declared the champions, it was no surprise to us.

Their performance had been nothing short of phenomenal, from the first round till the final round outshining even the physical education students. The History students stood tall, their victory a testament to their incredible skill and determination. "Peter…" my name was announced on the microphone the crowd started to cheer and the whistles were on everywhere, I made it to the stage and was appreciated by our principal who gave me a medal that engraved our college name "St John's College, Palayamkottai" with the logo of our college in it and a certificate of appreciation.

After the ceremony, we ventured to meet the faculty in our department. After some conversation about the intercollegiate sports event, Suki, our photographer, took some excellent photos of the occasion, including me with my medal and certificate of appreciation.

The bell rang and it was five in the evening. Since the college would be over at six, we guys had one hour left. We guys were chatting and having fun, while I was turned around, talking with Kanna. Suddenly, I could feel a person tapping my back. I just turned around and saw Muthukkumar, who was closest to me in our class. A good-looking boy, who's short but with a great personality and a genius too. It was a great surprise to me; I told him about the match but I didn't expect him to be here, as most of the time he will be on an OD (On Duty) to attend seminars and workshops.

He smiled and immediately said, "Pete I'm sorry, I tried hard but I couldn't make it to your game."

I replied, "Dude, that's fine... what about tomorrow?" My eyes lit up, and my ears perked up, eager to hear the words "I'm free Dude." The rest of the boys in our class had made a plan to go to Courtallam, as there was a local holiday in our district.

Muthukkumar replied, "Pete, have you forgotten that we both have a workshop tomorrow?"

As he said that all the smiles on my face faded, and I asked him if I could skip the workshop by any means. He reminded my word to him the other day to accompany him to that workshop as it was a long journey. Realising it was six passed five, we packed our bags and left our class. Once we neared the basketball court, I reassured Muthukkumar that I would go with him, as I always kept my word, and I did the same with Muthukkumar. With a little grief in my heart, I walked towards the entrance with my mates, and let the boys know that I couldn't be a part of their trip.

The group dispersed one by one, once we reached our college entrance which was made up of heavy black stones that looked aesthetically pleasing. Muthukkumar talked about our plans for boarding the bus, then told me that I had to be at the bus stand on or before ten-thirty. Suki came to pick me up. He waved at me. I too waved him back as he got on his bus.

The time flew faster than usual, as I reached home. My mom helped to pack my clothes and she insisted I keep a sweater, and the time was almost half passed nine to set my baggage ready. The time had been half passed ten Muthukkumar texted that he'd be in the bus stand about twenty minutes or less. After a short prayer, Dad gave me two five hundred. My mom intervened and asked my dad to provide me with more money. After he refused to do so she grabbed his purse and gave me a thousand five hundred. I hugged her and left for our car in the parking lot. It was a fifteen-minute drive from my place to the bus stand and Dad and I chatted about the competition. Then he reminded me that he had already booked a room inside the city, once we reached a person named Vinoth would be there to pick us up and he would arrange the vehicle for our workshop. Dad advised me to take care of my things and shared the number of Vinoth.

Muthukkumar was already there, so we went and inquired about the timing of the bus and waited there for about thirty minutes. We boarded the bus once the bus came, and as usual, he granted me the window seat. As we settled, I connected the earphones with my mobile, which played melodious music. I grabbed my bag and opened the front zipper where I kept a book that contained five short stories.

The Southern Concoction was the book in which I was fond of the narrating style of my professor Janaker Lawrence Daniel. After the completion of the third story, I found myself sleepy and had a good sleep.

The small flowers tried harder to lift their head but white clouds filled the whole place and the orangish-red ball couldn't make it happen on that beautiful morning and it made the buds harder to brighten theirs to the sky. A lady was working in the kitchen preparing some flavoured rice and the milk was boiling on the other side. The lady called her out but there was no response (shake or any movement in that thick bedsheet), once the tea was prepared, she placed it on a table and called by her name.

"It's already late, the tea is on the table, hurry up."

Slowly the woollen blanket loosened and a hand dragged it to the nose. The dark eyes rolled around the room and could watch her mother moving back to the kitchen. In a moment she turned the woollen blanket into a sweater-like thing by covering herself. Then she took the teacup and had a sip. It was pure bliss for the climate in Kodaikanal with hot tea. She was in a happy mood as the alarm sounded for the second time that morning. She placed the tea cup and stretched out her body. While she stretched out the woollen blanket surrounding her went down, wore a pink hoodie which was written as "a true love story never ends" Her teeth glimmered like pearls, and she made her soft curly hair into a high bun.

The light of the sun was dazzling, which made my hand move across and I could see the rays of the light flow through the narrow gaps of the eucalyptus and the rubber trees. Which was very beautiful and it was bliss for my eyes on a moving bus. As it continued and kept on continuing till, we reached the place where we had to.

We could feel the cold breeze and fog all around us. Before I could call Vinoth, Muthukkumar suggested that I wear my sweater. After a wait of fifteen minutes in a tea shop, we got our call connected with Vinoth. He said that he was already there waiting for us for more than half an hour. The time just passed eight, and after a twenty-minute drive, Vinoth helped us check into the hotel which was pre-booked the other day by my father.

There was no proper signal in the hotel, so we connected with the Wi-Fi after a five-minute struggle and talked with our parents. The door knocked persistently, as I opened the door Vinoth with the servers brought us breakfast. Vinoth asked the servers to keep the food on the table and asked me for any further assistance. I said, "If I need anything I'll call you, Vinoth." After Vinoth left I headed to the bathroom and came back as soon as possible, as the entry time of the workshop is nine-thirty.

She made quick adjustments to her appearance in the mirror, as the nearby church clock chimed indicating the arrival of the ninth hour. She hurried and grabbed the packed flavour rice from the kitchen and made her footsteps to the bus stop. The sky was then clearer than usual and it brought some happiness to her. She made it to the bus stop in five minutes, a green-painted local bus arrived on time along with her friend Rache she boarded the bus at sixteen passed nine.

Eventually, we arrived at the reception, Muthukkumar was asking about the timing of the bus. I told Muthukkumar

"It's almost nine fifteen, if we choose the option of going by bus it won't work out"

After Muthukkumar agreed with what I said, we opted to call Vinoth and asked him to arrange a cab for us. Once the cab reached the hotel we went on to the university on time. The university welcomed us with the statue of the "Iron Lady" of our country as it was written "Indira Gandhi Women's University" in the arch at the gate. After I saw the university's name, I came to know that it was a women's university.

It was located on the "Princess of Hills" Kodaikanal. As it was above the Kodaikanal hill station in Palani Hills, we could feel the cold breeze, but the sky was visible with no fog. The architectural dimensions were substantial, and moving from one building to another took time. There was a perspicuous view of the city, as it was situated at a higher elevation.

I got out of the cab as we reached the campus, and started to search for the tower range, as my hands were elevated facing the sky. The tiny bars in our mobile screens flickered for life as a human in his last moments. I've got calls from Suki, but the conversation between me and Suki is complicated and worse than we ever thought or experienced. Which made me mad at that time as he was on a work of mine in place.

Muthukkumar paid for the cab and we headed to the main building. There was nobody we could see in that building, after a while we saw a person walking on the other side of that building and asked about that workshop. He then showed the block where the workshop registration process was taking place. Our legs started to sprint as we could reach the five-hundred-metre range in a minute. On the front of that building they were serving some tea and biscuits, we're already full and went straight into the building where the registration process went on. The registration counter was placed in a hall, which was big but it looked like a vegetable market and it sounded the same. Nobody there didn't hear me crying out to move a bit to reach the counter. They were all doing their stuff like chatting and other things in the same place, I asked a person who stood near me.

"Bro why are all standing here, there are few who were registering for the workshop."

He replied, "The hall was not yet opened for the program, that's the reason, bro."

I nodded in a bit of confusion as to why they hadn't opened the place where they told me that the program was gonna happen at nine-thirty but it's almost seven passed ten.

After some minutes of struggle, we managed and made it to the counter, we're the last to do registration and stuff. There was a banner behind the registration counter, with the names of the guests and speakers of that day. One thing that I felt interested in was the name of that workshop "Research Rhetoric". Muthukkumar was filling out the forms and other stuff, I was beside him standing with my arm folded and looking at my surroundings. The girl who looked after the registration counter took two, I'd cards and placed them on the table.

The sound of laughter, conversations, and it reminded me of my school days when the whole class talked and the charge mam came and shouted "Is this a classroom or a fish market." Suddenly, two young ladies came into the hall where we stood for the past thirty minutes. They both started to set forth the people in the hall to the program area, among those two one looked different in my eyes, something had happened as I saw dark eyes with an eye freckle and dark eyebrows. With the blade nose and smiling pearls asked everybody to move to the program area. She wore a yellow chudi with some minute works and a blue stole which perfectly matched her. The black curly hair is braided and beautifully adorned. My heart pounded like never before, my brain was loading what was happening inside me in milliseconds. When I saw her after a year, I was so happy and I was speechless. I tapped on Muthukkumar's shoulder a couple of times, he replied in a frustrated voice "What's up dude". I jumped and said "She's here... she's here..." Is that "Mercy?"

And I nodded, as my face was brighter and glowed like ever before.

Our eyes had their first contact, ever since she finished her schooling. I wished that she would recognize me but it was a flipper on that day as she didn't even consider me as a person who did her work and moved forward a bit. Suddenly she made her soft steps back and excitedly looked at me, her eyes wide open with the black eyes with a blush on her face which took me back two years to the Mumbai railway station.

"The time was around half past seven in the morning when the train reached the station, and my friends went on a trip to Mumbai. We are walking on the fourth platform of that station with the trolly bags, backpacks, and other pieces of stuff. I've just noticed her on the fifth platform on my left, the moment we looked at each other, her eyes widened and she blushed and looked at me. Without the command of my brain, my right hand raised and waved at her, I was shocked at first. Then she waved at me back, which was the beautiful day of my teenage years."

She waved at me and asked through hand signals to be in the place of the program and she even tapped at her watch to indicate it was time and the program had already started. I nodded to what she said, as my thirty-two-tooth flashed like a bulb. As she was busy at that moment, she again pointed her to the program place to come quicker and left with her friend. Muthukkumar was about to finish filling the form but I felt like I was on top of mountains. Once the registration was over, we went on to the place where the program went on.

I went on with excitement, blabbering many things to Muthukkumar as we kept moving towards the program hall and almost thanked him nearly a hundred times for giving the name of that workshop. Muthukkumar asked something which shut me at that moment.

"Pete have you ever talked to her face to face,"

I instantly replied, "Dude, no matter what goes down today, I'm gonna look her in the eyes and tell her I like her."

He added something in response "What if she had a boyfriend?"

I had no answers for that question since our last chat was over months ago and I didn't know anything about her present on that day. We headed to the program hall. Once we entered, I looked around every corner and each row to see if there was any yellow churidar visible to my eyes. All my attempts to see her ended up in vain, to my left Muthukkumar was seriously taking notes on what the speaker had said. I took my mobile and started scrolling, then I opened my Snapchat app, where I found that she was online. I texted and she immediately responded, I asked where she was and she replied that she was in her class.

I told Muthukkumar "I want to see her now."

He replied "Why? Listen to the workshop, it's interesting." As we were on the last row, I grabbed and took him out of the program hall.

I said, "I want to see her otherwise, I'll never allow you to listen to this."

"Man, from the time you saw Mercy, you started to kill me. God..." He shouted in a frustrated voice and enquired about her class. Initially, I had a plan of seeing her through the window or by passing through that class. But there was quite a good surprise for us, which we never expected. We started to walk towards her class and could see our professor who left our college after her marriage. And then I got a chance again.

Muthukkumar and I went inside the classroom, and I could see Mercy and said "Hai" to her and she was like what... her eyes wide opened, and signalled "Mam" as her eyebrows went up. Mam was busy talking with the group of seven girls. Muthukkumar called her as she turned back, she was in surprise and her expression said that she was happy to see both of us. She immediately asked, "Pete is that you, attending a workshop."

I just smiled as my hand went to the back of my head, and then she asked Muthukkumar about his studies and other things as he was her favourite student in our UG times. As me and Muthukkumar were talking with our mam, I never took my eyes off her the whole time as she was doing some work. Muthukkumar tried to bring me back several times but it didn't work out. Then both of us came out of her class and Muthukkumar said

"Pete I was afraid about the things which you did in the class on seeing her."

None of his words entered my ears as my whole concentration was on Snapchat, as the discussion was about where we could meet and other plans. Beside me, Muthukkumar was in a rage and advising me on how to behave and other kinds of stuff, I just nodded my head at everything that he said and continued my chat.

It was lunch break, and still, we hadn't planned where to meet. I gave the tokens as they served the delicious plate of coconut rice, chickpea curry, and paneer masala with onion raita. I was waiting for her to be back online but she wasn't. As I was about to finish my lunch, she was walking towards the place of the program held accompanied by her friends, with a bunch of written certificates which she shared on the snap. I kept my plate aside and went straight to face her when she approached the hand wash area. Meanwhile, Muthukkumar saw my plate but not me and concluded that I might have seen her somewhere and gone. After a few minutes I came back, as my hands were washed, I had some excuses pre planned but he was not ready to ask all those silly reasons. Instead, Muthukkumar asked me "You've said the food is delicious, then what happened."

I replied, "Dude I was full that's why..."

He instantly said, "Oh, then who will take the plate..."

I said, "Sorry dude, my mistake."

He said "Just kidding man,"

"What did she say?" and put his hands over my shoulders and we walked towards the program place for the second and last session of that workshop.

The session went quite well for me, as she was visible, seated in the row in front of me. We had some conversations through hand and eye signals and a lot through Snapchat. She often blushed at me, which made me fall for her again and again.

The workshop was over by four, and after we got our certificates from the counter, we finally made it to the bus stop by half past four. The time kept on moving the clouds started to come down, Mercy was also there waiting for the bus, as the local bus arrived I along with Muthukkumar, and Mercy with her friends boarded the bus. She put her bag for me on the next seat of her. She called me by hand gestures, I hesitated as I looked at Muthukkumar he said "Go man" and pushed me to the front.

I sat next to her and my heart almost stopped for seconds and then it recovered and I could hear the sound of my heart. I was spellbound, but thousands and thousands of words bashing in my mind. I decided that it was time and we both tried to speak at the same time. After a minute and a half pause, I said "**Mercy....**"

A boy who looks elegant and chubby with curly hair hears a bold voice calling his mother's name. He pauses at the diary that he read closes it with a bookmark, and goes to the main door of the house. As he opens the door, he sees a man who wears khaki pants and a shirt with a letter in his hand standing at the front door of his house. The man asked, "Is this Dr. Mercy's house?" He said "Yes, it's my mother's name" and he asked what the person needed. The person says that he's a postman and he wants to deliver a letter to Dr. Mercy. The boy replies, "But she is at work in college, you can find her office number on this card." The man gets the card from him, which has the details and the office number of The Principal of the S.S. Government Arts and Science College, Tirunelveli. Dr. Mercy M.A PhD.

When the little guy turns the next page, it has all the answers. Not an **End...**

2. Beyond Horizons and Boundaries

The violetish blue sky welcomes the evening, Mr. Nagaraj, a lean old man with specs who's my assistant approaches with a file for signature. As I signed the circular for the pooja holidays, I insisted he inform the HoD's to share this circular with students through social media groups. The clock hits six, my maroon SUV is being prepared by the driver. I switch off my system but not the one that runs the surveillance footage. I quickly keep the documents and other pieces of stuff inside the locker which is spread on the table for the planning purposes of the new blocks. I take off my I'd card and keep it in my handbag, then turn the light and the air conditioner down. I just locked my office door and Nagarajan checked it for confirmation.

My office is in the centre among all the blocks, as I keep my out on the biometric the time moved around fifteen minutes. After some ten minutes, I went for a round in my car around the blocks. After that the car goes on the TL highways towards my home, I slide the window down and I can feel the cold breeze bashing on my face which takes me back to that day.

I was in the widow's seat after the driver's cabin, my hair was flying on the breeze. We were so close side by side that there was some strange feeling which was still difficult to explain and I was a little excited. My hair was falling on my face because of the breeze and the speed of the bus. As I adjusted my hair, we both tried to talk at the same time. There was absolute silence among us for a minute. I could see the tension and nervousness on his face and could felt that he was trying to say something I expected. Finally, he was about to say, as he said "Mercy", when the conductor of the bus interrupted us and asked for tickets. I was slightly annoyed then turned back to Rache who was two seats back, and said in a low voice "Ticket", she showed me the tickets, and he then said to the ticket collector, that it had been already taken by the person who's seated at the back.

After the ticket collector moved, I asked him in a little excitement "Pete, you've tried to say something!" He smiled a bit with nervousness flooding over his face and said "I... I tried to say, "Today's workshop was good, wasn't it?" I told myself "Oh! You have listened to the workshop, I have to believe that, poor Pete." He couldn't make a lie as real and the innocence in his smile attracted me in some way that was beyond words. I made a plan for a chill-out where we could explore some famous spots, then I asked him what time he had to board the bus to Tirunelveli. Then, he said it would be the next morning. I told him we'd explore some spots around this beautiful hill station. He agreed with his usual smile. I took my stole and covered my face then; we got down from the bus a couple of stops before the place where we took our tickets. After a five-hundred-meter walk, we went to a spot named Green Valley or the locals call it a suicide spot. There were shops on either side of the pathway towards that point and we both had some chats about the studies and other stuff. We bought some homemade chocolates and he took some pictures of me and Rache. There was an ice cream shop. When I saw the shop my eyes glimmered and I looked at Rache and smiled when I saw the shop. She immediately responded "Mercy, don't eat ice cream..." as Pete came with two pistachio-flavoured ice creams which were my favourite.

I grabbed the two ice-creams from his hands which Rache looked at and gave a reaction, where my mom's reaction could be better. Pete asked Rache if she needed ice cream she generously rejected and told me to get down to the entrance before she could finish her shopping. Muthukkumar was there taking pictures of the scenery and the monkeys around him. Pete got one for him and joined with me, we just leaned on a pillar and talked about the random stuff. Suddenly the clouds started to descend which was very beautiful and was done in minutes we couldn't barely see one another. Enjoying two ice creams in my hands for that kind of climate, was a different experience and I've enjoyed that climate, place, and company of my man.

I can feel the buzzing sound from my handbag, but the memories don't let me return to the present.

The clouds were high and the cold made him shiver. I took my sweater from my bag and gave it to him, which made him feel a little warm. Then we saw the frisky monkeys around us and our chat made the time move faster. There was a sign of Rache, as she was enthralled in shopping. My mobile rang, as it was my Mom I was a little nervous for a moment then answered that call. In a busy voice, she said, "Appa (Dad) and I are going to a marriage function in Dindigul and we'll be back tomorrow." She then told me to stay at my aunt's house, as she gave me the spare dress and my mobile charger there. We then moved to our houses as he and his friend went to the room to pack things for their journey. My mobile battery was almost at its end, so I turned off my mobile data. Rache said, "Don't fall into the trap, it's almost like you've fallen."
I told her, "You know my situation and it's not the way you

think."

"If it's not the way I think, then what does all this mean?"
Rache asked

"Rache, I like him and I accept that I've some interest in him. But that will not conclude that I had fallen for him. Moreover, I don't think this will ever go on to the next phase. You know me right, I don't have any belief..."

"I've not enough fortitude on my end to debate with you on this topic" She connected her earphones and turned her face towards the outside of the bus window.

I was happy and excited at that moment, other than that nothing stood on my mind. Then, I took my mobile from my bag, which only had five percent, I quickly on my data and saw if there was any text received from him on social media. After a few minutes of waiting, I thought he might not send messages till he boarded the bus. I pulled my quick menu, and my mobile vibrated with a coin flip sound. The notification "missing something, order now..." from the Tomato food app, raised my anger to the peak which led me to turn off my mobile. I went and knocked on the door but it wasn't locked.

The car takes a right turn, and as the gate opens by a watchman, the driver informs me that we have arrived home. He opens the door, and I grab my handbag and step out. Once I reach my doorstep, I remember something and call my driver.

"This weekend is off for you. Please, park this car in the college parking lot and pick me up on Monday morning as usual."

He nods, and the SUV drives away as the watchman opens the gate. I press the doorbell, but there is no response. I try again, this time calling out my little boy's name as I knock on the door. As I open it, a wave of fear surrounds me. I call out his name repeatedly, but there's still no answer. The fear creeps in from the corners, and I put my handbag on the couch and check every corner of the house to see if he's here.

I run toward the watchman, my hands shaking and my words trembling. My palms and feet are drenched in sweat; I can't speak as if someone has tied my voice box. Understanding the situation from my actions, he says, "Ma'am, don't worry. I'll search for him inside the compound."

Now I have some hope that he'll be somewhere inside the compound, but anxiety about his well-being runs in the back of my mind. My maid arrives at her usual time. Seeing me sitting on the steps with both hands on my head, she approaches, having learned the situation from the watchman.

"Madam, Thambi (which refers to the little boy) was roaming here and there inside the house, after getting bored by the TV he went on to the basement. I stopped him and then he went to bed by half passed one, after ensuring that he was asleep I went back to my house."

After I hear that we both directly go near the basement and try to open the door, but the door is locked from the other side. Watchman arrives with an iron rod and opens the door. I run as fast as I can down the steps and fall near him, as it is an old storage room filled with dust. I tap him on the cheek, calling his name, but there is no response. I see a diary that is half-read and his mobile phone near him. I lift him onto my shoulders, I can see a portrait full of dust carrying an image of a crowd surrounding a couple and run toward the garage, breathing heavily, and place him in the front seat, securing the seatbelt. My maid locks the door and rushes toward the car. As I open the lock, she jumps in, and the car speeds off, racing through the streets at eighty kilometres per hour. Once we reach the Healthcare Wellness Center, Muthukkumar is ready with a structure and a medical team. They take him to the Intensive Care Unit (ICU) because he has had breathing problems since a young age. He has been on medication since the day he came to me.

Time is passing by; he is still breathing with the support of cylinders. A sister gives the admission form to Rache, to fill out after filling out the form she gives that to me for the signature. I glance at the admission and fill the leftover place of my parents with my name. Muthukkumar's wife is a doctor, whom we've been looking for since the day I took him. She come and sit beside me and said as for now Ryan is fine but soon or less, we could opt for surgery as his heart is fragile. I can't control my tears, Rache on the other side rubs my back as my emotions take control over me. I lean my head on Rache's lap, she whispers some words of hope in my ears which strengthen me from the inside.

Time moves forward, and around eight passed fifty my eyes are drained without water, and many thoughts surround my mind. The doctor herself comes and informs them that they are shifting him to a normal room. In no time the room is ready and I can't even stand Rache giving her shoulder. He was brought by the helpers to the room in a structure as he is sleeping, and they transferred him to the bed. I place a chair near him and start to rub my little one's hair. Rache receives a call telling me she'll be back in an hour. His smiling in sleep takes me back to nine years on May twenty-seven.

It was my birthday that would conclude the first year of stepping out of my house. Then I worked as an Assistant professor in a college. I kept myself away from everyone and everything for that one year except one. The morning was a bit boring on that day, thinking of the memories with him. The milk in the pot was left on a high heat and it overflowed and some spilled on my leg. Then I came to a realisation and turned off the gas. It was already late for college as Karthika was also late. My mind shifted towards him. I could hear my little one's cry, the sound dragged me from the kitchen, crossed over the dining room towards the bedroom door of our house. As I opened the door, I could see my cute little master wearing a blue cotton dress wrapped with a white towel and little curly hair. Cried as his hands and legs were on upwards, his elegant face and the cute little voice of cry melted me. I knelt and cradled him in my arms, he suddenly stopped crying and slept in minutes. Whenever I took him in my arms, I never had a mind to keep him down, as Karthika came, she carefully took him from my hands.

I named my little King Ryan. Rache often asked me why Ryan, then once I said "Rache, did you remember the day of my labour?" In a low voice, she said "Yes", "I was taken to the labour ward after a visit to ICU, there was nobody except you and my sister." I didn't know what to do, or how to raise a child and many were bashing my mind after fifteen minutes of endurance, he came out. He was crying out in the arms of the nurse; I was dithered and then he was in my arms for the first time with the cute sharp little nose and less hair. As he was in my arms the cry stopped and a gummy smile bloomed, tears rolled out of my cheek and touched his forehead, that smile took all my pains and made me who I am.

The door of the room is open, as we are on a chat outside, which makes him wake up and he's sitting in the bed, with an innocent face. He puts his face down, and only his eyes search, me with some fear and love. I accidentally hook my head inside the room, seeing him awaken I hug him as tight as I can. Rache brings some homemade food for both of us, she scolds Ryan for going inside the basement without me. The clock hits ten, she gives Ryan a two-line advice and a kiss on his forehead which makes him smile. She comes near me "Don't worry about Ryan, he is perfect." And gives a hug and the door closes.

Ryan is in bed. I'm next to him, he asks me to tell stories, and I start the usual story. He intervenes "Maa, what happened after you reach home? Have you ever talked with Pete again? Are the Muthukkumar and Rache in the dairy the ones with us? Has Pete ever told you that he likes you?"

That series of questions hit me hard and I'm trying to figure out how he came to know all these. After a moment I remember a dairy was opened on the table as he was unconscious in the basement. My whole body is in a state of numbness and tears flow through my cheeks, he kneels on his bed and wipes my tears. He looks into my eyes "What happened Ma?" I said, "Nothing dear."

Our chats brought the dusk in no time, the usual alarm sung by seven after a regular bed tea I started to get ready for the college. The clouds covered the sun so that it couldn't spread its light on the land. I wore a green dress, and with my usual hairstyle, I made it to the bus stop after a five-minute walk. As I was ten minutes earlier to the stop where I usually board the bus, I unlocked my device and started clicking the keyboard on WhatsApp. I emerged on my phone as Rache came, I was unaware of her, for almost a minute she was behind me and when I accidentally turned back, I was caught. I smiled and tried to cover up, but she started to give me advice. My eyes could see her as an old lady who'll talk all "these, that and blah, blah...." Her class was echoing in my ears, as the sound of my ringtone reached my drums, I placed my hand on Rache's mouth and attended the call. It started to drizzle; we were in the shed at the bus stop. A voice spake in a clear and crisp manner, "Turn your left Madame". I immediately turned left, and there I could see a man under an umbrella with camel-coloured woodland shoes, wearing a blue chino and a white colour shirt with stripes. With a classic watch with a blue strap on the left and a khaki-coloured shopping bag, he was lean and had a little beard with a moustache. I was charged a bit and that day I felt that old me was back, he came near me and handed me that shopping bag. At that time, we were a bit familiar, but it still required time for us to utter a word through words but our eyes...

Ryan starts to cough and I take some warm water in a glass and just incline the bed a bit. I try to give him one instead. He gets that from me and drinks the water, I rub his back and chest to make him feel comfortable.

He then asks "Mommy, then..."

From that day on, our chats extended through calls and social media. He was the kind of guy who would back down for me if there was ever an issue; we had our fair share of fights, but they never felt serious, just lots of "sorry." Those little moments of happiness, arguments, and cute surprises made our connection special. We tried to meet up several times, but it never worked out—he always gave me space to do my own thing. Sometimes, he would get a bit wild from the pressure and stress which could lead to saying things that contradicted what he had said before. Then he'd apologize for it, which I never liked, and I'd call him an "idiot." He made me laugh, and of course, I made him laugh too. Time flew by but our care for each other remained as it used to be. I always had an idea that men weren't reliable. He showed me otherwise. Those were the happy days that we spent in the company of each other.

A year passed after we met at the workshop, usually Summer was the time of the season on Kodaikanal. Every road in the city was full of cars, buses, and bikes. Many took the way of walks to reach the places inside the city and some took rental cycles to explore. The city overflowed with people and the government had given some rules and regulations for people to follow. It was a usual day for me. I was accompanying my mom to the market, and I was texting him amid the heavy crowd and it started to drizzle, which indicated the commencement of the pre-monsoon but still the people were busy with their shopping. My mom was busy exercising her skill in bargaining with an old man who sold carrots, my right hand was typing something to my friend and the left had a grip on a bag that had some vegetables. Someone accidentally took out my bag and I got a little angry. I turned on that person and stared for seconds and said idiot which did not louder. That person was away for a foot. He turned and looked at me. He wore a black mask with a woollen sweater and came near me and said sorry. The voice reminded me of him, as he was half kneeling and taking the bag I looked into his eyes, he winked and took his mask on one side and it was him. I was stunned, my heart started to beat fast as my mom was near, at that same time I was very happy and blushed at him. He then put on his mask and followed me wherever I went in that market, although we chatted through social media our eyes spoke more than our chats. We had a friendly relationship for almost a year, but at that moment, a rush of emotions hit me like never before and made me realise that I was falling for him. My eyes were flooded with tears, but I managed to calm myself down. I received a text once I reached home, which stated "Hey, there is a box which was wrapped in a paper. Check that!!" I put my mobile on the bed, ran towards the kitchen, and took the shopping bag to my room. Mom came in no time and asked me "Mercy, where is the shopping bag?" by asking that her steps start to walk towards the bedroom. As she came, I was having a carrot and chewing and another carrot. On the other hand, she smiled at me and told me to wash and eat the carrot, then took that bag and left the room. There was a great sigh! I texted him and scolded him for keeping the gift without letting me know. He tried to convince me but I scolded him by text message. I let my head out of the door and peered if there was danger around me and it was the perfect time to go. I opened the box that had some of my favourite chocolates which I'd mentioned to him long before in our chats.

Once we met in Kodaikanal, we met again in a few months as I went on a trip to Shillong with my classmates for my college tour. It was a four-day trip in Shillong and the fourth day was the most important day of the whole trip. I was very excited about the place and it was my dream to be there. Rache and I were the closest among the seven of us, on the whole trip we guys were separated from the rest and enjoyed the most. All seven of us were united whenever we went shopping, on this enjoyment of my favourite trip I had only less time to talk with him. I could feel that he was upset with me, but I tried my best to talk to him. Somehow, we managed to talk for five to ten minutes a day, as most of the time we were on the spot, sometimes we were on the travel. On the last day, I woke up early as it was so cold I went to the balcony of my room. The whole place was covered in fog, I kept myself warm by a navy-coloured sweater and a cup of tea. The Scotland of the east is well known for the "cherry blossom" which was my favourite part of the whole trip. We took a bunch of pictures and for our last spot we went to the place named "Police Bazaar". I was tired cause of the restless roaming on the spot and I didn't eat properly that whole day. We made it to a restaurant and finished our dinner, as it was the tourist attraction time the prices were a bit high. Traditional dances and many other things were going on the streets. Rache and two other friends of mine took me by saying "There is a famous dessert shop which is famous for their ice creams." I felt a little exhausted after that dinner but the vibe on the street was enormous. People were dancing on either side of the streets; the streets were decorated with lighting and a music band was on one corner of the street.

Rache asked have you talked to Pete this evening, I said no and asked did he say anything important. As I took my phone out to call him, the music band played my most desirable track and the people in that bazaar started to dance around me and I was baffled. Rache left me in the middle and joined the group to dance as my other two buddies did the same. I had a feeling something was about to happen. As the band sang, "In your eyes, I see the light, my future," he suddenly appeared, leaving me in shock once again. He was in blue jeans, paired with a charcoal blazer and a white T-shirt, a flower bouquet in his hand. He was nervous and trying to say something, I was still confused about "why did he come here, is he going to propose to me" While those questions struck my mind the people around them were very curious by taking their mobile phones out and focused their camera on us, the people talked to themselves as "he is going to propose her. Will she accept him and many more..."

He came near me, as the song was mild in the background mixed with the cold air. He gave me the bouquet; my heart became warm as the words started to pour out from his mouth. "You're my favourite person and we've shared so many laughs. Now, it's time to make a lifetime of memories. Will you be mine forever?" My family and other problems of saying came for a moment in my mind, but my heart kicked them out. Tears started to flow from my eyes like a waterfall and I couldn't speak. I started to cry and hugged him as tight as I could.

That was the first time we said that we had feelings for one another.

After that trip, when I got back, a bigger problem awaited both of us. We tackled it together, and those challenges only made us stronger. We had plans to leave home together, he went to the airport as planned and then boarded, but without me, the plane crashed. I've never found any information about him since. Six months after Pete went missing, I finally stepped out of the house, after seven frenzied months that's when you, my little prince, came into my life and shaped me into who I am today.

I still believe that he is still alive...

3. Memory of His Touch Once Again

At three o'clock, the blanket loosens its grip on little Ryan. He slightly opens his eyes and glances around, then slips off his bed, carefully watching his steps as he moves toward the window to see if the orangish ball in the sky twitches its head. Since it's dark outside, he returns to his bed. The conversation between Muthukkumar, Suki, and Mercy from that night fills his mind, giving him a puzzle that swallows his sleep. Ryan wants to know who they are talking about, but he remembers something about the ICU.

Once again, he slips off his bed, puts on his slippers carefully, and moves close to his mom to check if she's in a deep sleep. After confirming that she's still sleeping deeply from exhaustion, he drags a chair near the door, causing a grrrrrrhhhh sound. After a minute of dragging the chair, he feels relieved that she hasn't woken up. As he climbs onto the chair, Mercy stirs slightly in her sleep, making his heart race. He waits for a moment, then unlocks the door and successfully slips out.

Looking both ways down the corridor, he walks through, his usual fear of hospitals creeping up on him. He's always been treated at home whenever he gets sick, and this is the first time in about five years he's been to a hospital.

"Madam, the patient moved his hand a bit." Hearing the news Dhanam, the chief Doctor runs towards the ICU. Seeing the patient, they can feel the difference in him, the doctor talks with her colleagues "Soon are less we could see him recover and it's a happy news, inform his family." Dhanam comes out of the ICU and sees Ryan staring at the corridors and she can see that he's searching for something. She is extremely shocked at seeing him, and runs near him "Ryan kutty, what happened? Why were you here? Where is Mommy?" The series of questions made Ryan fumble a bit, he struggled to answer her questions "Doctor Aunty...." She understands that he is ready to know what happened...

He takes him back to the room, as Mercy is searching for him in the corridors on the next floor. She calls her back to the room by the ward boy, she tells Ryan to sleep and when Mercy comes, she shows her signals not to speak here as he fell asleep just now. Dhanam calls Mercy as they go to a place on the same floor and lock the door from outside as Ryan sleeps. After a quick nap Mercy wakes up at seven, Ryan is still asleep. Rache comes early with some tea and breakfast for both, with a cup of tea Mercy tells Rache a health update which brings out fresh smiles on the faces of both.

Muthukkumar comes to see Ryan while Mercy is busy with her call. While Muthukkumar and Ryan are playing, he asks questions that stun Muthukkumar often. Suddenly, Ryan asks Muthukkumar, "Uncle, did the plane really crash?"

"Ryan, which plane are you asking about, Uncle wasn't sure kiddo."

"So, the aeroplane crash which Mom told me has not happened. My Mom just lied to me, uncle."

As he says these he is reminded of the words of his wife "Babe he is ready." In seconds he again, asks a question, stating

"Why did Mom never let me talk with Dada over the phone? Uncle, I can remember a person in a hospital who never talked or did anything but slept for hours with a mask, which I often used."

As these questions are like bullets, he continues.

"Uncle, can you take me to my Dada?"

As Ryan asks this question, tears stream down Muthukkumar's face, and in a blubbering voice, he says, "I'll show you your Dada." Rache, who is standing nearby, wipes her eyes and softly says, "Go..."

Rache is swiping her mobile through Google Photos, Mercy comes in after her call and asks Rache about Ryan, she replies "Ryan was bored and asked Muthukkumar to take him outside for a walk." As she sits next to Rache, Mercy starts to check on her work.

After some minutes of silence Rache asks "Mercy, did you remember this picture?"

The picture captures the important day of Mercy and Pete, where familiar faces from both sides come together to share in that lively and joyous moment.

On seeing the picture, she smiles as the glance of her eyes shows how she enjoyed that moment. Rache asks her again, "Hey, did you remember the happenings of that very day?" This question made Mercy dive deep into the memories of Pete, which takes her back to October 3...

"After that trip to Shillong the Police Bazaar moment came to the ears of our houses which made things more complicated for us. That was the time that tested our budding but the understanding and cooperation between ourselves made that thing look easier for the people who saw us from outside. But those were tough days for us in every possible way. We tried for almost a year to convince our families. They were somewhat happy for Pete to become part of the family, but ego played a role on both sides, making them stand firm in their decisions. Both of us were completely frustrated, so we decided to make our relationship official through the bond called marriage."

Muthukkumar carries Ryan in his arms to the ICU, where a man lies, his body connected to tubes at every possible point. He makes Ryan stand near the bed, Ryan gets down and looks at Muthukkumar the face Ryan says that he is in fear of seeing such many tubes in a person. Muthukkumar grabs a chair and places it near the bed, lifts Ryan, and makes him sit on the chair. He is a little nervous and silent, which unmatches his character. Muthukkumar walks near a cupboard opens a drawer, grabs a diary gives it in his hands, and sits on a couch in the corner of the room. Ryan turns the pages as it stated

It was heavy rain in the hills, Muthukkumar was getting ready with a maroon shirt and a white dhoti. Rache came with an umbrella although she was half-drenched, Muthukkumar gave her a counter which she responded with a tap on his back head. And advised him not to act as a groom, as we laughed and hi-fives around ourselves. I grabbed a cover, which contained a pair of boxes. I grabbed one for mine and gave the other to Rache. As she reached the front door of that house, waved and indicated to us to be sharp at ten-thirty in the register office, there were other friends with me for the signature of witnesses. The emerald green shirt she picked out fit me perfectly, and I paired it with a pair of tailored black trousers and a pair of shoes with a silver chained watch. Prem, my dearest friend, returned from abroad for my marriage. Although the roads were filled with water from the rain and the hills were drenched, I felt a great sense of hope within me. One in our group asked about the date, Prem tore the paper of October 2 and it changed to October 3. He was the first to remember my birthday, wrapping me in a hug and sending his best wishes, after getting wishes from the boys. I turned on my mobile data and saw a flood of messages from my sweetheart wishing me a happy birthday at the start of the day. After a twenty-minute drive, we reached the register office by forty passed ten in the morning with the anxiety of getting late and being berated by her. As Ephi was driving, he parked the car at the parking area and we ran to the old looking building before we could get drenched.

Ephi, Prem and Muthukkumar went inside the office and came after a minute and said they were not there in that office. My anxiety got over and I started to sweat heavily, Prem tried to make me calm as we started to try their mobile phones but then it was the part of the signal that pushed us into deep frustration. The time was running and the assistant of the registrar gave us multiple warnings to be on time before twenty-five passing eleven. Prem and Muthukkumar went on with the hope of initiating the formalities inside the office, a black colour jeep splashed the waters and entered the premises. It was parked perfectly in the parking lot, as the left door opened a black umbrella came out, and a foot stepped on the ground with a closed-toe sandal wrapped with a pink-bordered silver-coloured silk saree with some works on it in golden thread matched with a pink jacket and with a gold chained watch. Accompanied by her sister and Rache, as she came near me, she gave the umbrella to her sister, took her handkerchief in hand, and wiped my sweat. At a distance of fewer than twenty-five centimetres, my nose sensed her fragrance, her thick eyebrows, and her black eyes made me think anything for her. I grabbed her hand, pulled her towards me, then put my arms around her waist, looked into her eyes, and asked "**Will you be mine forever**" The moment I asked the question, her cheeks turned pink, and she gave the cutest little nod, blushing hard. It made me fall for her all over again, Prem whistled to bring me back and a signal that we were good to go. The registrar asked her if all of this happened of her own free will, and she nodded in response, making the registrar *take the register and mark the place to sign, she took the pen kept the point on that paper, and looked at me as the black magnets were filled with waters of joy. I gave her a smile she signed, followed her I signed the register after the witness's signature was signed it was made official.*

I stayed in the hills for almost half a month, we met often with her friends and sister's help. I planned to settle in London, where I could find a job that matched both of our qualifications. Initially, she refused to do so, but later I convinced her and went back to my place to move on with the visa process. Months passed by once a month, I went there so we could meet and have a good time together. It was a usual thing between us after that trip, she was the one who used to call and I was supposed to call or message her back. That particular week I didn't receive any call or text from her, I tried Rache multiple times but couldn't reach her. So, I went to Kodaikanal on my bike. Somehow, I contacted Rache and asked her to bring Mercy to our usual spot.

*Rache brought her, on seeing her made my life back in me with a sigh. I was a bit angry and when she came near, I raised my voice and she immediately hugged me as tight as she could and tears rolled out of her eyes, that spellbound me and she never left me for more than half an hour. She looked up into my eyes and asked **"Do you want us to become a family?"**. I thought that as usual, talk and tell if that's God's plan surely. She immediately loosened her grip on my waist, grabbed my hand placed on her stomach, and said **"I can feel him"**. When she placed my hand and said those words, I was the happiest person on earth, I was speechless for minutes. At that meeting, we planned that we have to make our visa process faster so that we could avoid unnecessary problems.*

Now, I have so much work to do for us... Still, I doubt in my mind how she is so sure that it's him, anyway we already chose a name for him **"Ryan"**.

Ryan turns to the next page, only to find it empty. He looks at Muthukkumar with a dimmer expression on his face. He calls Ryan to sit beside him on the couch and tells the rest.

"I was preparing to step out of my house, but our plan was alerted by someone. I was in a situation to be in the house, that's why I asked my sister to convey the message to him. She made multiple attempts, and the last call got through, he immediately asked if we had reached Chennai. Just as she was about to say the problem, she could hear the people scream from around and there was no response for a long time. The next morning's paper explained to us clearly what had happened to Pete on his way to the airport. On seeing the news in the paper my heart almost stopped, I started to breathe heavily, and it lasted for minutes until my body went numb. When Rache came to visit me that morning, after being aware of my situation she gave me first aid. She called Muthukkumar, and he explained the whole scenario and confirmed that he was alive and he's in a coma. Dhana who's the wife of Muthukkumar and the chief doctor Health Wellness Centre took charge of him from then. A couple of months passed and I started to feel it was difficult to go into the path, with the help of my sister and Rache I stepped my foot out to a new world with more mysteries,

sorrows, and happiness.

Ryan gets off the couch and moves closer to his Dada with a bit of hesitation, starts rubbing his palm, as he tries to pull his hand away. Just then, Pete's hand grabs Ryan's pointer finger gently...

"Ever heard of crime? Curious about crimes? ...Yes, we know. Coming soon in the form of novellas..."

-GARJ